"Pancho raised his broken body from the burnt West Texas soil,
'Take my stetson Lefty,
Take my stetson, and ride,' he whispered.
A posse of thirty men were just beyond that horizon.
Lefty stood fast, he knew the time was near.
Pancho slumped lifeless to the red clay with the words;
'Think of me Lefty' on his lips.
Lefty, loyal to the last, blessed himself, removed Pancho's
stetson and replaced it with his own battered sombrero.
He mounted up, and with a cry of,
'Ride with me Pancho,
Ride like the wind!'
He thundered off, alone, accross the flat-lands towards the
Morning Star........" (Pancho and Lefty's last stand.© 1997)

This book is dedicated to all the Leftys of the world, for their loyalty in the face of adversity, especially dearest Fiona.

I would like to thank Connie Pa, Blake, Ollie, Tom McCarthy, Austin and Moira, Gerry and Aidan (Fr. Matthew Street), Sylvia (Uppercase) , Con Collins and many others too numerous to mention (in a paperback edition) without whose help and support, this collection would not have seen the light of day.

Pancho & Lefty Ride Out

A Collection of Short Fiction

 Cónal Creedon

THE COLLINS PRESS

Published by
The Collins Press, The Huguenot Quarter, Carey's Lane, Cork.

The Publisher wishes to acknowledge the financial assistance
of The Arts Council/An Chomhairle Ealaíon, Ireland.

Printed in Ireland by
Colour Books Ltd., Dublin.

Book Design by Upper Case Ltd., Cork.
Typeset by Upper Case Ltd., Cork

ISBN 1898256063

CONTENTS

*COME OUT NOW! HACKER HANLEY is based on fact, it being the only non-fiction story in this collection. The events and characters involved are true in every detail, to the best of my recollection...

Born in Cork 1961, Conal Creedon lives in the heart of Cork city, where he runs a launderette. A prolific writer, he has written many short stories, plays, monologues, radio plays, T.V. scripts, and his ever popular, mad-cap, surreal radio drama *Under the Goldie Fish* (R.T.E. Radio Cork) which has, to date, clocked up over 200 episodes and was lauded by the critics;

" The gist of Under the Goldie Fish would make Gabriel Garcia Marquez turn puce in a pique of jealousy."   *(Sunday Tribune)*
"Radio highlights of 1994."   *(Irish Times)*
    "Scripts and characters as bizzare as will be found anywhere."
        (Cork Examiner)
Creedon's mad plots,......make this little programme a joy."
    (Irish Times)

Over the past three years, Cónal has achieved recognition as a fiction writer, his stories have been published extensively in various periodicals, broadcast nationally (R.T.E.1) and have won many awards, including prizes in The Francis McManus Awards and The George A. Bermingham Awards. At the present time, his story *Come out Now! Hacker Hanley* is being adapted for animation and is in production.

Cónal is currently working on a novel, and is planning his first venture into film making.

Pancho and Lefty Ride Out! is Cónal Creedon's first collection of short fiction to be published.

And the Big Fish Drowned

Finny raised the hammer again and crashed it down on Macker's head. His skull burst open, like a freshly boiled potato. Blood flowed freely across Macker's face, and seeped through his faded Wranglers at both knees, his right arm lay awkwardly over the kerb and onto the road, as if it had two elbow joints. Blood trickled down his Wrangler jacket sleeve from his shattered forearm and dripped into the gutter. Macker was silent.

"Don't ever make a langer out a' me!" Finny roared.

"Do you hear me!

Don't ever make ..."

Finny was about to repeat himself. The door of 'The Greyhound' bar opened.

"Jesus, you've murdered him, Finny."

Drinkers poured onto the street.

"Bastard!" Finny shouted.

He squeezed the handle of the hammer, swinging it at the gathered crowd, roaring senseless aggressions. They were not entertained. A look of reality returned to Finny's frenzied face, he hardly recognised his best friend as he lay there feeling no pain. Finny dropped his hammer hand to his side, raised his head towards the orange street lamp and howled.

"Bastaaaarrdd!"

Finny turned and ran off, into the dampness, up Castle Street. The 'China Garden' and 'Paul's Plaice' shone like beacons, that was the way, and there was the light. Around the respective yellow and cream glows could be seen the faint images of people coming and going, like flies to a lamp. It's said, there's no life without light, well, in this part of town there was no light without life, where even the dullest of street lamps would have a cluster of people. They chatted, sang, shouted, fought, made love and then they went home.

Finny was cold and sweaty by the time he reached the flats at the top of Castle Street. He passed down behind the park, through the fence at the back of the flats, and over the wall into the school yard. In the corner of the shed he lay down on the bench, the blood dripping hammer by his side, he fumbled for his Major, took one out and lit it. His heart hammered out a regular but loud beat, so loud, that his ears, chest and toes pulsated to the rhythm. His stomach was in a knot, he had a pain in his cranium.

"Bastard deserved it," he thought to himself, and sucked in the blue smoke through his nose, as it bellowed from his jaw-hung mouth. By the time he had smoked his second fag, his breathing was back to normal and his thought process a bit more rational. Finny realised he had gone a bit over the top, after all, Macker's only crime was that he grabbed Finny by the nose and dragged him around The Greyhound.

"Say after me," Macker taunted. "Macker is the Boss!"

Finny obliged, but it was the last straw.

"Bastard made a fool out a' me!" Finny was heart-broken.

"The hammer! ... Why the hammer?" Finny questioned himself.

"Maybe Macker didn't deserve to die, but he definitely deserved a good hiding."

He raised his Doc Martens up onto the bench and lay back, sucking tobacco.

Finny smoked, the smoke rose and settled, calmly it filled the shed.

"This shed is full," thought Finny.

"full of memories."

It was here on this broken bench that Finny and Macker first experienced life. Finny smiled. He remembered lazy days balmin' out on the roof of the shed, in their underpants. He remembered nights of getting the gawks, getting it on, fumbling with bra straps and getting it off. He remembered Macker's first kiss, it was with Jacinta Healy in the corner of the shed, the two of them stood there with their tongues in each others' mouths while Finny, sat in the far end of the shed, slugging cider.

"Man! Oh man! Ya gotta try it Finny dis is what it's all about, boi."

Macker was in his element.

Finny was happier with his lips around the neck of a cider bottle than his tongue wrapped around Jacinta Healy's tongue; the very thought of it made him shudder. He pulled his bomber jacket tight around his rakish adolescent frame. He felt cold, he felt lonely, he felt strange sitting there in the shed, alone, no laugh, no crack, no Macker, just himself and the glow of his cigarette. Finny was heartbroken.

Deep down, Finny had seen this day coming. All was well while they were drinking cider, having fun but when money and dealing ten spots of dope came in the door, personalities became more exaggerated and fun and friendship went out the window.

Macker wanted drama, money and danger, Finny wanted friendship. And when Macker began to see himself as an Al Capone type figure, the friendship had to stop, something had to give and Macker got it outside 'The Greyhound' that night.

Finny knew that if Macker was dead, he was in trouble, but if Macker was alive, he was in big trouble. He decided there and then that he had seen the last of Cork, there was nothing here for him anyway. He pushed himself up off the bench, walked out of the shed, flicked his butt across the yard and threw the hammer as far as he could over the roof of the shed, into the undergrowth. Back over the wall, down past the flats, up the hill homeward, he was on the boat to England the next day.

Macker didn't die that night, he earned a limp, but this only added to his street cred. In the years that followed Macker grew into the biggest fish in the small pool by the Lee. He did 'time' when he was in his early twenties, but this gave more fuel to the myth, the enigma, this man called Macker, better known as the Boss.

The Boss was the MacCavity of crime. A house break in the northside, an armed robbery down town, a shooting in the southside, the Boss was never found. As always, the myth was larger than the man. He was a liar, a lout who sold drugs to minors through minors. He drank too much and, with no self-respect, he abused all those around him, especially those close to him.

Jacinta Healy was still with him. He married her about a year after he acquired the limp and, three months later, she had his child. This was a time when Macker was at his most lovable, most vulnerable. He missed Finny, his body and heart hurt. But, in the years that followed, Macker slowly regressed into the pig of a man he was. He screwed around, messed around, hung around. Hanging around, with hangers-on. That was Macker. He lived in a world of ten spots, touts, back-handers and back-stabbers, but he was the Boss. Surrounded by a bunch of no-minds, his 'organisation' grew from strength to strength. Money was easy in the drugs game. Buying in bulk, through the Molloys, a well-organised gutter family from Dublin, he sold on through a system of hangers-on to kids. Simple. No banks, no tax, no paperwork, no problems! When a problem did arise, someone would get their head burst open and the problem would go away. Macker busted heads, no problem! But it was this very simple principle of the law of the jungle that brought Macker down.

The law of the jungle had only one principle, might is right. Don't mess with fat cats. Small fish got busted, especially if they showed initiative. These men were animals. And when Macker's body was pulled out of the river there was no question in anybody's mind, it was the Molloys. It all added up, Macker messed with the Molloys, Macker was dead.

Macker had dealt with the Molloys for over twenty years, buying quantities and selling down the line, everything from hash to heroin. Heroin was never a very big runner in Cork, but Macker had it on his menu. A point of prestige, showing the Molloys that, in Cork, he, Macker, was the Boss. The Molloys knew where to buy, how to buy. They had the hardware and people to bring the stuff in. Here lay Macker's dependence on the Molloys. Macker, 'The Boss' was a small cog in the Molloys' well-oiled wheel.

But the 90's brought change, change to Macker's fortune. This change was brought about with the introduction of one little letter, 'E'. Disco biscuits, or better known as Ecstasy, had arrived. 'E' hit the scene and Macker supplied it. He dealt directly with England, no middle men, no Molloys. 'E' was small, 100 hits would fit in a fag box, and, at £25 a hit, you're talking two and a half grand a fag box. Profits high, risks low, no middle men; 'E' was big.

Macker was ambitious, but ambition in the drugs game had a domino effect, where one move affected all. One man's gain was another man's loss. Joe Molloy was that other man, and he wouldn't take loss easily. Molloy's blood was up, and Macker's was spilt. The 'D. S.' sighed a sigh of relief with the death of Macker. 'Misadventure' they said, but everybody knew ...

* * * * *

"Gimme, Gimme, Gimme !
A man after midnight. "

The jukebox thumped it out. ABBA were back and so was Finny. Twenty-three years had flown by and Finny was back, back for Macker 's funeral, back for the funeral of a man he would have gladly halved his heart for, back for the man he would have killed.

The smell from the toilets soiled the air. Finny rubbed his nose, it smelt of tomcat and stale drink. The C. D. and big screen were new, and the extension with the pool table and jukebox gave the place a different appearance, but 'The Greyhound' was still the same, same smells, same heads, same dump. Finny paused in the doorway, the place was jointed. He stepped into the bar, followed closely by his partner and business associate, Trevor. Trevor was young, in his early twenties, well dressed in a black polo neck, a light Armani jacket and black trousers, he looked sharp, Finny looked around the bar. He was looking for a familiar face but he wasn't recognised.

Through the crowd came a hand of friendship, Jacinta Healy, Macker's widow.

"Finny?" she reached out, across the painful years.

"Jesus Jessinta! I'm very sorry for your troubles. We flew over when we heard the news."

Their hands clasped emotionally. Over twenty years had passed since they sat in the school shed with Macker, supping cider. They talked as if it were only yesterday. She offered him a drink, he accepted a mineral water. Jacinta wouldn't know a Rolex from a durex, but she knew Finny looked well. She commented on how well he looked. He stood there in his Gucci and designer labels, tanned and trim. The years had obviously been rough on Jacinta so he cut the small talk and sympathised. She was consoled.

"I don't miss that shagger, I loved him, but I don't miss him," her eyes were cold.

"Mrs. McCarthy," a hand from a hanger-on reached between them.

"I'm sorry for your troubles. The Boss was a great man."

Jacinta nodded, the hands shook, parted, the hanger-on released his grip, and walked away.

"Ye had a son?" Finny continued.

"Yea, Junior, that's him over there." She pointed to the brat pack by the pool table.

"Is he a good lad?" Finny mentally picked him out.

"He's good to his mother." Jacinta smiled.

"Good." Finny nodded.

Trevor stepped forward to offer his condolences.

"Don't I know you? Haven't I seen you before?" Jacinta studied Trevor.

"We may have ..." Trevor was about to answer.

"I know you!" she continued

"You work for the Molloys. You supplied the Boss." Her eyes flashed anger.

Finny, seeing the potential for trouble, stepped in.

"You got it wrong Jacinta." he reassured her.

But she wasn't convinced.

"He's one of the shaggers who murdered my shaggin' husband. Finny, he murdered your buddy!" She began to lose the head.

"Jacinta, ya got it wrong." Finny firmly held her arm. "Come outside, Jacinta, you're upset. Let me explain." Finny pointed her in the direction of the door.

"Explain?" she shouted. "Explain dat shagger."

Finny led her out of the pub, onto the street.

Outside, Castle Street was still on the wrong side of town, buildings boarded and pavement battered. Finny held Jacinta by the shoulders. She leaned against his waiting limousine. She stood there dazed. He told it as it was. He talked of Macker in a way that no living soul from Cork had ever spoken. He spoke of Jacinta's life as if he were there for every tear drop. He spoke of Junior and the life he never had. He spoke the truth, and for a woman who had heard a life-time of lies, she readily accepted this truth. These truths she knew to be true. He then went on to explain his unorthodox business relationship with Macker, and how in all Macker's dealings with Trevor, Finny's identity was always kept secret. He told her of the early, lonely days in London, his rise through the ranks of the drug world, and how he was bigger than the Molloys. Finally, he told her straight, that the whole story of Macker's murder by the murdering Molloys was nothing but myth making and Macker was laughing all the way to the gates of Hell. The Molloys had better things to be doing than messing around with small fry like Macker. If the facts were known, Macker had probably fallen over a quay wall in a drunken haze, on one of his drunken bouts, and good riddance.

"Don't you say that." Jacinta's eyes flashed. "Sure you tried to kill him, yourself, twenty years ago."

She saw glory in death, and Macker's myth was the only pride she had. But Finny had said all he could.

"Ah for shit sakes! Are ya not listening to me? Me and Macker were like that." He raised his two fingers, clinched together.

"I loved Macker, girl. Trevor, I'm outa here, shag her! Shag anyone who looks like her!"

Finny sat into the back seat of the limo and slammed the door. Trevor held Jacinta's wrist.

"Who the hell do you think you're holding." Jacinta looked daggers.

"Look, Mrs. McCarthy," Trevor was gentle, "we came to offer our sympathy, and now . . ."

"Shaaagg her!" Finny shouted from the limo.

"We have a plane to catch, get in the car. Shag her!" He was close to tears.

"Mrs. McCarthy?" Trevor shook Jacinta's wrist. "Please accept this."

He slipped her an envelope. Inside, a wad of cash, three grand, sterling.

"It's from Finbarr," he whispered.

"Finbarr?"

"Finny!"

She smiled as she made the connection, she had heard Finny called many things over the years, but never Finbarr. Knowing her meal ticket was gone with Macker, she calmed down and listened to Trevor. Trevor made it clear that Macker's link in the trafficking chain would have to be filled. He suggested Junior.

"Junior? Drugs?" she was having none of it.

"He's dealing already and you know it." Trevor rationalised.

"It's in the blood, let him join the big league."

"And what about the Molloys? I'll have another corpse on me hands!" Jacinta needed reassuring.

"The Molloys are nothing!" pleaded Trevor. "Finny would eat 'em for breakfast. He feeds the Molloys. Finny is 'The Boss'

Jacinta stood there confused. Trevor slipped slickly into the back seat of the limo.

"We'll be in contact!" he dropped a cliché.

Jacinta's eyes filled. Trevor cradled Finny and rubbed his hair affectionately, Finny's cheeks were streaming.

"You're a bastard, Finny White. Macker always said it, a shaggin' steamer." She grabbed at him through the window, as the limo drove off.

Finny cried like a baby, unashamedly.

"Don't worry love ...it'll be alright ..." Trevor caressed Finny's hair, and kissed him comfortingly on the forehead.

"It'll be alright." he reassured.

Orange street lights flashed over head. Finny watched through watery eyes, as Castle Street became more and more removed from him. Jacinta faded in the distance and, with her, the emotional hold of youthful memories. The ghost of Macker had been laid to rest.

"Trevor?" Finny sniffled. "Did I ever tell you about the time me and Macker broke into Tommy's Bar, jez dat was de night, ye see we were walkin' home along, and .."

Finny was off on a "me an' Macker" story. Trevor smiled. He had heard these stories a thousand times, both from Macker and Finny. He had heard them call each other every name under the sun, but always with respect and a strange affection. He knew that, deep down, his lover, Finny, had a special place for Macker in his heart. The nostalgic separation of twenty years only served to enhance their mutual respect and affection. Trevor was jealous of something he would never understand. This jealousy was a problem for Trevor and, in his circle, problems were solved by breaking heads. The ghost of Macker had certainly been laid to rest, no problem!

To the humming of Finny's story telling, Trevor assessed his future dealings in Cork now that Macker was out of the way. He looked forward to his new partnership with Macker's son, Junior. Junior seemed like a nice chap, cute, nice bum too. Trevor looked to the future. The limo purred as it cushioned them from the hacked surface and depravation of the southside. Finny, occasionally turning to glimpse out the back windscreen, rambled on, reliving legends and creating myths. Trevor, eyes front, smiled as the crest of the Mercedes guided them through the damp, smoky mist that always hung on Castle Street, up past the flats, down by the park, behind the schoolyard and up the hill to the airport, homeward.

Limbo Junction

Did you ever wake up with 'Waterloo Sunset' running around your head? Well, that's how it was.

> *"Dwang diddy dwang!*
> *Diddy dwang!*
> *Diddy dwang!*
> *Diddy dwang!*
> *Diddy dwang!*
> *Bab ba ba ba ba*
> *Ba ba ba ba ba ba*
> *Ba ba ba ba ba*
> *Ba ba ba ba...."*

You know how it goes? Well, that's how it was.

* * * *

Ding! Dong!

Spring was late, two and a half years late to be exact. But the light was beginning to shine through.

Ding! Dong!

There it goes again.

It was for one of the other flats.

Nobody ever called for me. I'm more the visiting type than the host type.

Ding! Dong!

Jesus! Will someone answer the door!

People were forever ringing the wrong bell, my bell.

You see, this house has eight flats, sometimes seven and a studio, that depends on Herman, our resident German. When he's flush he usually takes Number 6 as a studio. Studio, if you don't mind. A flat is a flat, is a flat...a bloody studio. Some people - really!

I mean, it gets to the point where the rest of us, including Willie the Rent, call Number 6 'The Studio'. A bloody joke, that's what it is! I'm the ground floor flat and, by some inexplicable technical feat of electrical wiring, the top door bell...strange. Actually, when I think of it, this house has only seven or eight flats and yet we have twelve door bells, and not one of them with a name tag except, of course, Number 6 which has in artistic scrawl 'Studio' stuffed in behind the yellowing plastic I.D. holder. Is it any wonder I don't have many visitors?

Ding! Dong!

"Jesus! Will someone answer the bloody door?"

I buried my head deeper down between the gritty sheet and grubby cover...deep down into the darkness, a winter darkness. Somebody famous once said that the light at the end of a tunnel was probably the light from an oncoming train, that's how I felt. But I was beginning to sense a new beginning, or was it the beginning of a new end?

The Land of the Midnight Sun...that's what it was like, two years of sunshine followed by two years of darkness. And darkness is a strange thing, so passive. It's just the lack of sunshine. Darkness doesn't do, it just is. At least the sun has to shine, but darkness sits there doing nothing - just being dark.

It had been a long dark winter and there was some class of a lunatic outside my door, ringing my bell!

Ding! Dong!

The duvet cushioned me from the ringing of bells, the laughing, the footsteps on the ceiling, the insanity that manifests itself outside my door in the dimly lit hallway and the sinister madness outside the front door, the door out onto Waterloo Terrace that looks out across the schizophrenic estuary of the city. It was dark down there in the duvet, my knees curled up to my chin. It was musty, damp and airless, but it was safe...

Ding! Dong!

"Answerthefuckingdoorwillyaanswerthefuckingdoor!"

Depression? Call it what you like, but I was safe. This was my second stint down under the duvet. I remember the first time, it seems like a lifetime ago. Then again, maybe it was, and if not a lifetime it was certainly a different life-form, 'cos I have changed.

* * * *

She was young, I was younger. She was French, from Montpelier. I was travelling north on my student Eurorail ticket. North to Germany and then South to Italy but my money ran out in Amsterdam, that was where I first clapped eyes on Yvette. She was sweet, sophisticated, sensual and working in a café/juice bar just off Damrak. I can't remember the name of the place, in fact, there's a lot about Amsterdam I don't remember, but I remember Yvette. She was tall, slim and firm. She stood there behind the counter, near the cooler, cigarette hanging from her lips, talking to her workmate, a taller girl, a taller black girl, from Africa or Germany or someplace. In fact, it was the Afro-German I first noticed, hard not to notice a six foot two black woman with a flame red skinhead. She was wearing a pale blue halter-neck, sort of a boob tube thing, that barely held it all together and shorts so short that they just about covered the junction of her legs, legs that ran curvily all the way from counter to floor. I think I was in love, real love. I just wanted to go to bed with this exotic vision, not that I wanted to make love or anything. I stood there, five foot ten, a twenty year old virgin as she leaned over, her crotch caressing the counter mounted bottle-opener. Well, maybe it wasn't caressing the bottle-opener but it just seemed that way to me. I wanted to marry this girl, I wanted to take her away from all this, I wanted to save her from herself, save her from all the leering eyes. I wanted to...

> "I want to hold your
> ha-ha-ha-haaaaa-aa-nd,
> I want to hold your hand,"

The Beatles zapped crystal clear from the hi-Tech C.D. jukebox. "Vot do you vant?" Her lips puckered not three inches from my forehead.

"Pawpaw." I wasn't too sure what a Pawpaw was but I knew it sounded hip, I knew it couldn't be much different from an apple or an orange. She eye searched the shelf.

"No Pawpaw" she raised her hands in the air, they in turn raised her arms, which in turn raised her shoulders and in turn her halter neck top. Down dropped her melon-like bust line, revealing a sleek chocolatey brown board-like stomach, untarnished except for a wrinkle of a navel. God, I really, really, really, really loved this girl.

"Mango?"I sucked my stomach in.

"No mango!" She didn't raise her hands.

"Papaya?" I knew I was making an impression.

"Papaya? No papaya." this time she didn't even search the shelf.

"Melons!" I spouted, the next exotic fruit that came to mind...

"Listen sunshine, don't fuck me around, what do you want?" Actually, now that I think about it, I'm sure she was from the north of England, Newcastle or someplace like that.

"Whatever ya have," says I, trying to be amiable. She presented a menu and walked off, her shorts riding higher and higher into the crease of her buttocks.

"Ah yes, menu...now let me see...Holy Saint Finbar!" They had everything, red Lebanese, Morrocan black, blonde, green, every colour hash under the sun, they had weed, grass, tops, Thai sticks, heads, big flowery heads.

Now, my drug experience up to then had been fairly limited. I may have had a puff or two of some class of grass, or something like that, but really, the whole dope scene was something that just totally passed me by. Call it peer pressure, call it what you like, I didn't want to walk out of that café without making a purchase. I looked down the counter. The black girl was talking to the, as yet unknown to me, Yvette. She pointed in my direction.

Yvette swayed up the counter, I grinned hopelessly at her black friend.

"Bonjour" she didn't smile.

"How's she cuttin'?" I guffawed.

"So, do you see anything you like?" she hissed in that inimitable French

13

way.

"Yer friend!" I left a yahoo out of me.

"Pardonnez?" She stood there looking confused.

I looked at the menu.

"Eh, what's the difference?" I shrugged my shoulders.

"Well, obviously ze price, but...." then she proceeded to explain the relative merits of the different colours, scents, textures of hashes and grasses on the menu.

"Zis one will bring you up,
zis one down,
zis one smooth easy,
zis one very happy."

"Have ya got one that will blow the head offa me?" Looking back, I suppose that was a stupid question.

"How you mean?" she looked puzzled.

"Which one is the best?" I clarified.

"Zere is no best, zere is no better, it is all excellent."

"Look," I explained, "I want to do some real brain damage," I knew this would impress her.

She produced a ready rolled joint, "I suggest you smoke zis, a leetle only, yes?"

Her maternal instincts had surfaced and handing over a handful of guilders, I winked and smiled at her tall black friend.

"And a cup of coffee, a good strong one...yee outcha boi ya!"

I sat down, lit my joint and waited for my coffee.

"Ra-ra-Rasputin..."

It got louder and louder and louder,

"Ra-ra-Rasputin, lover of the Russian Queen."

I sat there for what seemed like seconds or hours, I'd never know. Everything was so clear and incomprehensible at the same time. It was hell, it was heaven, it was Boney M.

LIMBO JUNCTION

"Ra-ra-Rasputin"

...and it got louder.

Suddenly everything made sense, the 'why' of life. The answer to the unaskable question (and it does matter if that tree falls in the woods). I sensed my spirit, my life force, my raison d'être. I could see my soul, it was there on the back of my hands, pink and white dots beavering away all over my body like ants. It was fascinating. Turning to the palms of my hands, I watched as my soul filtered away back between the gaps of my fingers, back behind the hairline of my wrist. My skin tone changed from red to purple and the veins, buried deep inside my hands, rose to the surface from blue to black. The skin gave way to a trembling pulse of raw fleshy, sinewed foul meat that dripped, lard-like, from my cupped palm to table. I held my festering molten hand over the ashtray and sat there in horror, watching the fluid flesh drip. Attempting to scream for help, all I could manage was "ugh!"

I couldn't manoeuvre my hands, my head or avert my eyes from the unfolding surlifeism as my left hand painlessly, gorily dripped into the dirty ashtray.

"Ra-ra-Rasputin!"

And then the most uncontrollable urge to go to the toilet. I remember learning somewhere the biological term for the muscles needed to hold the faeces inside but I can't think of them now and I certainly couldn't think of them that day, in that café off Damrak. Anyway, I somehow managed to make my way to the toilet. I sat there for an eternity, watching the portafleck paint play cowboys and Indians as the world fell out of my bottom.

Knock! knock!

"'Ello, 'ello, everything is alright in zere?"

It was Yvette.

I sat there staring at the toilet door, as this Cecil B. de Mille-ish western unfolded before my eyes.

Limbo Junction

For once the Indians seemed to have the upper hand, but that was probably due to the fact that they were securely stationed inside the circled wagons. While the cowboys rode feverishly around in circles outside, a whoopin' and a hollerin', shooting into the air and generally making a nuisance of themselves, the Indians just crouched there taking pot-shots, picking off the cowboys one by one. And then, just when it seemed that the cowboys were well and truly licked, there came a fanfare. It seemed to emanate from the door latch. I concentrated on the minute dots, expecting to see the mandatory Company of the 7th Cavalry charging, blue steel flashing to the rescue, but no, not at all. It was a host of saviours, but not a blue coat in sight, nor red coat, now that I think of it. This band of gallant light cavalry charging to destroy, or to their own destruction, was an elite corps made up of the heroes of all the displaced nations of the world, riding to the sound of the guns. They rode in an orderly fashion to the rhythm of their triumphant war harps. I'm sure it was something from the Ó Riada Mass or maybe Micheál Ó Súileabháin. Anyway, who cares, it was glorious just to sit there watching as the anti-heroes of the world charged to the rescue of the Indians, who were actually winning anyway. They were all there, all those who had fought the good fight and lost. Asians, South Americans, Aboriginals of all casts, even the Dali Lama was in there with his regiment. And out in front was a squad of men and women under a green flag emblazoned with a golden harp, the Irish, led by James Connolly on the left flank and Countess Markievicz on the right, screamin' for blood. For once I felt sorry for the cowboys, but then again, it was so refreshing to see history being written by the vanquished.
Knock! knock!
"'Ello? 'Ello?" in the distance.
Everything was blurry, I don't know who won the battle, in fact it could be still raging there on the back of the toilet door in that café off Damrak. Whatever about that battle, I think I know who won the war.

How I left that cubicle is a mystery to me. On my feet or on the flat of my back, I'll never know. All I knew was that, I woke up next morning in the arms of Yvette, feeling airy and free and no longer a virgin. Not that I can remember any of it. But that was how I met my wife.

Those were days of dreams and ideals, a future of a happy-ever-after, poetry. The sun shone down on where we walked. That was before the darkness set in for the first time, that was when all in the world was beautiful, young and good.

* * * *

Ding- Dong!
"Jesus!, Somebody get the shaggin' door!," I screamed into the mattress.
Thump, Thump, Thump, Thump, on the ceiling.
"Pluto!" a muffled scream through the floor boards, "will ya answer yer feckin' door!"
It was Brenda, the brasser up in Number three.
Now, I don't know for sure if Brenda was really a brasser or not. I couldn't swear on my mother's soul to it, but everybody called her a brasser.
Strange thing, a name. Everybody calls me Pluto. I even called meself Pluto but it's not my real name. Noel McCarthy, that's my name. Always has been, always will be just plain and simple Noelie. Well, that was until they started calling me Pluto. Don't ask me why but it was a name that stuck.
Ding-dong, Ding-dong.
My bell again.
Thud, Thud, Thud, Thud.
"Pluto! the feckin' door!" Another muffled scream.
"It's not for me, Brenda. Answer it yerself!" I roared.
Tap, Tap, Tap, Tap.
"I can't believe this." The phantom caller was at me shaggin' window. I pulled my head up from under the heavily scented covers...a pot pourri of fish heads and socks.
Tap, Tap, Tap, Tap.

"Wrong bell!" I roared.

"Ring another bell!"

And then, silence.

"Thank Christ! Peace at last!"

I pulled the covers around my ears, right hand reaching out for a Major.

I fumbled it from packet to mouth and then,

Click!

of my Bic.

I drew in deep and the cleansing, life-giving smoke stretched my lungs.

My right hand replaced the lighter on the upturned orange box, fingers finding the switch on my clock radio.

Tick!

"And bringing you to the news at eight and what it says on the papers, here is the Duet from the Pearl Fishers."

It was John Creedon on Radio One.

I lay back, sucking my Major, smoke bellowing from my jaw-hung mouth, flicking the ash into my coffee mug. Well, it wasn't so much a coffee mug as an ash tray. No doubt it looked like a coffee mug, you know, mug shaped with a handle and traces of soured coffee, but it hadn't been a coffee mug in about two, two and a half weeks. Since then it stood, coagulating coffee at the base, next to my clock radio, an ashtray, an almost full ashtray. It was more subnormal than surreal, it was like I was acting a part but the plot was going nowhere.

Ding, Dong.

"Fuck off!"

Thud! Thud!

"Pluto, the fuckin' door!"

Tap, Tap, Tap, Tap.

"Ah, Jasus, this is ridiculous!"

So, I threw on my overcoat to cover my prudishness and slipped into my untied boots. I placed my hand on the handle of the door that led to the bulbless hall, the hall that led to the front door, the door of the bells.

Knock! Knock! Knock! Knock!

"Is there no peace in this world?"

I jerked open the door.

"What!" I was on the offensive.

There, in the darkened hall, stood Herman, overalls daubed in layers of coloured paint, canvas overalls better than any canvas I had seen up in his bloody studio.

"What Herman? What do you want?"

"Your door bell, ja?" He stood there up to his neck in continental arrogance.

"Look, why don't you open the door, you're nearest it," I smiled smugly.

"Is your bell, ja?" No budge out of him.

"Just 'cos it's my door bell, don't mean 'tis my visitor. It's probably for you, Brenda or the Monk."

"Ja! Ze Monk!" Herman reassessed his position.

Jimmy, or the Monk, as we called him, lived up in Number 4, a Neanderthal in his late forties. He had spent half his working life on the roads and building sites of England. A tough life for a tough man but at the delicate age of forty-five he returned home, unable to keep up with the rat race of the building line. He first came to live in our house about two years ago and ever since he was was in the process of refurbishing his imaginary cottage out in Carrig na bhFear, Carrigaline, Carrigadrohid. Well 'twas Carrig a something. He had a habit of collecting bits of broken furniture, cracked toilet bowls and non-reflective mirrors from skips around the town.

"For the cottage," he'd growl.

Everybody knew there was no cottage and that he was flogging his bits and pieces in the second hand shop down on George's Quay. The pile in the hallway got higher and higher. Anything the Monk did never bothered me. I had enough insanity behind my door than to be worrying about the madness in the hallway.

* * * * *

Ding- dong!

"Pluto! Answer yer bell!" It was Brenda the brasser.

"It's O.K. Brenda, I'm in the shagging hall."

I stood there in my boots and overcoat getting the last blast of nicotine into my lungs.

Ding-dong!

"Will ya get it Pluto?"

"I'm getting it, I'm getting it, don't get yer knickers in a twist!"

I looked up, she was like a mushroom induced vision, she stood there at the turn of the stairs in her pink fluffy slip and flip-flops, pink satin viscose-mix dressing gown, her peroxide beehive down around her ears and, like me, she strained to get that nicotine hit from a well-burned butt.

"Ah, how are you this morning, Brenda?" Herman smiled.

"I'd be an awful lot better, Herman boi, if he'd answer his fucking door bell!" She pointed at me.

"I was just telling Herman that it might be my door bell but it's not my visitor," I explained again.

"And what's more," she snarled, "what about all that rubbish in the hall?"

Brenda always had a problem about the hall, I suppose it affected her clientele.

"Well, it's not mine," I defended, "that plastic bag there is mine but the rest," I looked at Herman, "well, eh, I don't know."

"Don't look at me," Herman protested. "O.K! O.K! This big chunk of wood here is mine. I make a sculpture in the back yard, yes?"

"But all this things here, phaaa!" Herman threw his arms to the bulbless light fitting.

"Actually, I'm sure most of that stuff is the Monk's," I added.

Enough said, Brenda had enough on her own mind than to be getting involved in the tangled mess that contorted and distorted between the Monk's ears.

Ding! Dong! Ding! Dong!

"I comin', I comin'," Herman shuffled towards the front hall door.

I stood there transfixed.

Brenda, her head bent to her waist and turned sideways in an effort to catch a glimpse of the visitor from her obstructed view at the turn of the stairs. I swayed from heel to toe with an "I told you so" arrogance, sucking my cigarette. Nothing but an overcoat and and old pair of boots to conceal my nakedness, now that's arrogance.

The front door opened, a dazzling brightness silhouetting Herman.

"Eh, is me Dad there?" a small voice asked.

"Your father?" Herman echoed. "Who is your father?"

Good question Herman, good question.

"Is that you Veronica?" I moved to get past Herman.

"Oh Dad! I'm glad, I wasn't sure if this was the right house!"

"Jesus, Veronica girl!" I buttoned my overcoat. "Come in, come in! What brings you up here this time of the morning?"

* * * * *

This was an awkward one.

Veronica isn't really my daughter at all, but Mags, her mother, was my ex-girlfriend, or more like my ex-ex girlfriend, 'cos I was out with another girl since or, should I say, while I was going out with Mags. I know, I know. It confuses me too, but what can I say. Hey, that's life.

You see, when I first met Mags, I was coming from Limbo. I had reached the point where I had stopped struggling with the loss of my wife, the beautiful Yvette.

When Yvette walked out of my life it was goodbye to naivety and hello to cynicism. I realised that the prince didn't necessarily marry the princess and I suppose sometimes the princess might have to kiss a few frogs before she meets her prince. And as for this "they all lived happily ever after" bit....forget it!

But now I had no Yvette, I had no future, that was when I first found myself deep down under the duvet, deep down in the darkness.

Two years there, two anguished years of drink, disillusion and delusion, I fell down a lot and woke up in the most unusual places. Two years of head space, two years of insanity, out of body, out of mind, out of head. It was my Limbo and Limbo does exist. It's the absence of supreme love due to ignorance rather than any misdeeds...that's Limbo for ya.

Not such a bad place...it's a place of total objectivity, it's a place where you are free, free to float around in your ignorance. It's a place of self-assessment. But it doesn't last forever; it only seems that way. Like drowning, when you stop struggling you just float gently back to the surface and all is hunky-dory. And, as I say, that's when I first met Mags. She was an unmarried mother and I was a wifeless husband. She was a Liberal. A bleeding-heart Liberal, with right wing tendancies... left of labour, right of Fianna Fáil, you know the type, I suppose if I were in my right mind I wouldn't have touched her with a 10 foot barge pole. But my mind was far from right. I had just been blasted head first, without a helmet, through the barriers of a broken marriage in holy Catholic Ireland. Yep! I thought Mags and her little girl Veronica were the best choice at a bad time. They moved into my place and I moved into their life. It was good while it lasted. I'm not bitter or anything but, "shag her and anyone who looks like her," is all I can say.

* * * * *

I looked down.There stood Veronica with a face more beautiful than Mag's.
"Eh, come in, Veronica love."
"Thanks Dad." She was always a mannerly child.
Brenda the Brasser vanished back up the stairs, in a lurex flash of pink while Herman hovered around my door saddle.
"Do ya mind, Herman, I'd like a word with me daughter."
"Oh, by all means, by all means," but there was still no move out of him. So gently, I slammed the door in his face.

There I was in my overcoat and boots standing in the middle of my kip of a flat, with a young girl who insisted on calling me Dad. Veronica stood there, mouth opened and wide-eyed. Odd really, she was the first stranger, and when I say stranger I mean person living outside our house, to cross my threshold and, having my hovel viewed with a new set of eyes certainly opened my eyes and nose. There was a stench of rot about the place. It was like a bomb had hit it.
"Jesus Veronica girl, good to see ya. How's yer Mam and everybody, eh?" I was unnerved.
"Here la, excuse me manners, eh, take a seat...take a seat."

And, like Norwegian Wood, she looked around and, you guessed it, no seat. (I'm sure Paul McCartney could put it better but you get my drift.) So I lifted the coffee mug-cum-ashtray and clock radio from the orange box.

"There la," I pointed.

"Thanks Dad." She was never one for small chat.

"Eh, Dad, it's Eddie's Confirmation today and Josephine asked me to come up and remind ya."

Now, this is where it gets confusing 'cos Josephine, like Mags, was an ex-girlfriend. In fact, Josephine is the ex-girlfriend I had been out with since Mags. And Eddie, he's Josephine's son, what can I say, I'll never be sure about him. They all said I was his father, but really, I'll never know.

Veronica stood up to leave.

"I suppose I should be getting back and giving Mam a hand." She was never one to hang around. Herman could take a leaf from her book.

"Well if ya gotta go, ya gotta go!" I made it easy for her.

"So, will we see ya later?" She wanted confirmation on the Confirmation.

"Oh, chalk it down, Veronica girl, but eh, where exactly is the Confirmation?"

"Eh, the North Chapel!" She boomeranged it back. It was as if I was supposed to know these things.

"And, eh, time?" I tempted fate.

"11 o'clock." She went to leave.

"Eh, Veronica girl?"

"Yes Dad?" She turned.

"Eh, what date is it today?"

She looked at me as if I were an imbecile.

"It's the 23rd of April, is that good enough for ya!" she looked through me and turned to walk away. I followed her to the hall door. I mentioned the Dole and the fact that I'd meet her up at the Confirmation, after I signed on.

"Look!" She stood with brazen face. "Be there early, be there late, or don't be there at all! Do you think I give a shit! I'm only the messenger."

Not a girl to mince words, our Veronica.

"Ah, no, no," I giggled nervously. "I'll be there, I guarantee ya," I reassured.

But I don't think my guarantees or reassurances counted for much, not with Veronica anyway.

"Eh, see ya later so Veron!"

"See ya Dad!"

She raised her hand in a dismissive wave.

I watched Veronica saunter out of Waterloo Terrace and down into the filth of the city, a woman before her time.

After the Ball

Down our street change comes slowly, so slowly, in fact, it's undetectable, undetectable like aging, yet inevitable. Some things never change, and, as usual, there was Tommy outside my counter, scrounging a free read of the 'Evening Echo', before he headed home.

Outside the traffic was thick, spluttering out its heavy metals, heavy metals that made their way up to the second floor windows and stuck like tar. Through my shop window I could see frustrated faces, facing home and no move in the traffic.

"The traffic is a bit of a joke," I looked to Tommy for a continuation of the conversation.

"Nothing new about that. I'd say Cornwall Street was ass to nose with ox in Viking times!"

A car door opened, the driver got out, his car still in traffic but going nowhere, just ticking over. The shop doorbell announced his entry. I stood up.

"Fags for me nerves," his eyes scoured the cigarette shelf. "20, ... ah ... hem, Carroll's," he pointed.

It occurred to me that he had been off the cigarettes, and had just broken out. This man was obviously under pressure.

"The traffic is cat ..." I said being sociable.

"Cat?" he raised his voice. "It's down right diabolical!"

"Cornwall Street is always diabolical," Tommy butted in.

"A bloody bottle neck," the driver continued.

He went on about two lanes coming into three and then lights at MacSweeney Street, followed by another two lanes or something to that effect. I took his money, gave him his fags, said thanks and sent him on his way.

Outside, traffic had moved about ten feet up the street. Red heads had emerged from car windows behind my customer's car.

Horns honked, fists flaked the air, followed by the odd roar of abuse. The cigarette smoker got into his car apologetically, drove ten feet up the street and stopped.

It struck me that, Cornwall Street might have been ass to nose in Viking times, but it wasn't always that way.

"Would you believe that we played eight-a-side soccer up and down that street without interference from traffic and that wasn't such a long time ago." I pointed in the direction of the hotel gate.

Tommy dropped his 'Echo' about six inches and raised his head.

"Well ya wouldn't play pickie out there now."

I made my way back to the window and looked out at the madness.

The stretch of road between the gate into the hotel car-park and the gate next to my Father's shop was our stadium. The roar of the crowd that echoed inside our heads would sometimes burst out through our mouths in the event of a goal, foul or near miss. You'd find us there every day after school, funting the ball up and down the street, shouting, roaring and red-faced.

* * * *

It was about quarter past four, coal smoke filled the air, the sky dark, the street badly lit. About nine of us had gathered around the street light like flies, standing, sitting, shoving.

"Someone call over to his house and get the ball!"

I stood up from the kerb, threatening to go home.

"There's no way his Mam will give out the ball without Marbles."

"Well, someone call over to his house and get Marbles!" A pause - no volunteers.

"Hang on! .. I thinks I sees him."

"Dere he is!"

"Dat's him!"

And there he was over by the Blood Bank, ball under his arm.

"Hoi Marbles!"

"Come on!"

"Kick the ball!"

Marbles could hear us but he was still out of range. As he crossed the lane near the tea shop it became clear why he was late. Trailing behind him was his baby brother, Paudie. Marbles wasn't talking to Paudie but Paudie was out to play.

"Come on Marbles! We're waiting! "

He passed the corner by the pub and raised his right index finger in the air, as if judging the wind direction. He walked out onto the street, the ball moved mysteriously from under his arm onto his outstretched left hand, his pace quickened to a trot. The ball dropped and, without missing a step, he gave it a lash. It shot like a rocket up above the street lamp, into the darkness.

"Trap it!. ."

"On the head!"

"Chip it in!"

"Lay it on!"

A quick warm-up, the teams picked, and the game was on.

We had an uneven number of players that evening so, as always, Marbles' kid brother, Paudie, would be a floater. A floater was basically a player whose duty it was to even the teams and, in the event of a goal, the floater would have to suffer indignity, change sides and play for the losing team. It seemed to me that Paudie played most games as a floater. You see, he was really a hopeless player, probably due to his age, or lack of it. We did feel sorry for him, but the facts of the matter were that nobody wanted Paudie on their team. Night after night Paudie would be out for a game. It was pathetic seeing him turn around, dejected, and play with the losing side, while his ex-team-mates jumped and howled to the sound of the Kop, North Bank or Stretford End. What a way to start life. Always on the losing team, a born loser, trying to even the odds, that was our Paudie. What he lacked in skill he certainly made up for within effort. Paudie would spend the whole game running his little heart out without even as much as a smell of the ball, except when it went wide and ended up in the hotel car-park or down the lane. Paudie was the one who would run after it, anything for a touch of the ball.

It was coming towards the Angelus. Most of us had to be home, it was time to call it a night. We were tired and sweaty, the score was 14 all.

"Next goal wins!"

The rule was on, the ball out, and the pressure off. All men forward, we were playing attacking defence. The next goal was the only goal that mattered.

A quick break, a clatter of sparks from quarter irons, roaring, backward running, tugging, shoving. A scorcher brought the Stretford End to their toes.

"Ooohhuuaagghh!" in anticipation.

The ball clipped the footpath, spun in the air, bounced and was going wide, keeper had left it off. From nowhere came Paudie, his little knees thundering like pistons under his short pants, his right leg shot out awkwardly, left knee drawing blood as it scraped along the road. The ball made contact with his ankle, it rebounded off the footpath and bounced. We all stood there, rooted, as Paudie tumbled over, flat on his face with the sheer momentum of his effort, the ball spun and bounced, and bounced again. Keeper was caught flat-footed. He could do nothing but watch as the ball bounced beyond him into the goal!

"Goal! Goal! Goal!"

The Stretford End was in all its glory as the word 'Goal' echoed from gate to gate around the stadium, followed by the chant.

"Give him a ball
and a yard of grass,
Paudie'll leave you, on your ass!"

His mouth ajar and his eyes like saucers. Paudie made a dash inside the keeper, picked up the ball, raised his right hand in the air and waved it to the invisible crowd behind the goal. He jumped in the air shaking his little clinched fist. The excitement was at frenzy pitch as we milled around Paudie, hugging him and shouting. Marbles ran up behind his little brother and rubbed his feather-like hair, with a father-like pride.

"Doubt ya Paudie, boi!"

Paudie was peaking, not only was he on the winning side but he also scored the winning goal and he couldn't be sent to the losing team. The game was over. He, Paudie, had won the match. Paudie, ball in hand, was on a lap of honour, as the rest of us made our way to the gate for our jackets and jumpers. Paudie would talk about this goal for weeks, all he wanted to do was to get home and tell his dad, he would remember this moment 'til the day he died.

* * * *

To the screech of brakes, I turned. The ball shot up the street, and Paudie was under a bus. None of us had seen the bus. Little Paudie certainly didn't, sure hadn't he just scored the goal of his life. I have vague memories of neighbours on the street, with prayers and tears and me and my buddies ushered into the back of my dad's shop. I didn't really understand the meaning of a closed casket funeral, all I know is that I never saw Paudie again. Paudie, the floater, was gone.
Marbles' family moved out of the street soon after that, and, of the other nine boys there that day, only one remains living on our street; me. I can't remember some of the names of the boys who played back then, but I do remember that day, vividly. It was the day we lost the game, it was the day street soccer became a thing of the past, the day Paudie was killed. .

* * * *

It was dusky outside, and the traffic had moved on another few feet Tommy folded up the 'Echo' as neat as he could and put it under the pile on the counter. It was almost six o'clock and he was heading home to catch the news on the T.V.
"I was reading that the Corporation has plans to pedestrianise this street." he placed his hand on the door handle.
"This street?" I questioned
"Yeah, Cornwall Street."
"'Ya, serious?" I drew back from the window.
"Yeah, the traffic will be moved around on the Link road, up the quays and back around into MacSweeney Street. It would be nice wouldn't it... it would be nice to have the place pedestrianised." Tommy paused and began to button his coat.
"Dis place was pedestrianised long before there was traffic on it. They

never got planning for the traffic!' My back was up.

I could see Tommy was getting uneasy so I dropped the crusade.

"I suppose it would be lovely ... you know flower pots, a few chairs, that sort a' stuff."

I continued.

Tommy shoved his sandwich box inside his coat and headed off into the dark, home to his gas-coal effect fire and telly. I watched him cross the street, weaving in and out through the traffic and pass over beyond the pub, the pub where Marbles had kicked the ball from his hands all those years ago. I knew, pedestrianisation or not, I would never kick a ball on our street again. I also knew my children wouldn't, not only because of traffic, but because there was nobody left to play with. The families had moved out, out to the Corporation reservations on the north side, out of the heart of the city.

I could see the faint outline of Tommy over by the old Blood Bank, now a carpet store; he passed the lane where Marbles used to live.

I remember some of the boys' faces, and names who played back then. I rememberd the day Paudie died, vividly. It was the day street soccer became a thing of the past. It was the day the traffic won the game, and the heart of a city stopped beating.

Every Picture Tells a Story

I suppose my happiest days were when I was just being myself, hanging around.

* * * *

"Veeronniiccaaa! Do ya hear me? Veeronniiccaa!" she'd scream.
The gallery would shake.
"Maaam! ... Are ya lookin' for me? ... Maaam! ... Where are ya?"
The gallery would quake.
"I'm up in de top gallery! Veronica? Can ya hear me? Veeronniiccaa, I'm up here!"
And from the sculpture gallery, two flights down, a predictable reply.
"Wha? Maam! I can't hear ya! Where are ya Maam?"
Mary had been cleaning these halls for over half a life-time, and now she was in the process of training in her teenage daughter, Veronica. Everybody knew Mary, she was part of the furniture. She was known for her wit and sincerity, but by those of us who were new to the gallery and didn't have the years behind us to build up a relationship with Mary, she was better known for her lack of colour co-ordination. With her hair tucked up under a checkered head scarf, and a 'Gaudi' yellow, acrylic polo neck peeping out under her blue-red floral nylon dust coat, her white sports socks over her brown tights and fluffy slippers. How could I forget her fluffy slippers, they were the talk of the gallery.

Cigarette hanging from her lip and buckets and brushes and mops hanging from her hands, Mary would manoeuvre around the gallery, dusting, sweeping and mopping. Dusting a frame, she'd notice her own reflection in the glass, seeing her face surrounded by the frame, she'd stop, adjust her head scarf and move along.

The clip-clop-clatter of Veronica's teenage, black patent, sling back platforms announced her arrival across the well-worn teak-block flooring.

31

"Do ya want me Mam?"

Mary looked up:

"Jesus, Veronica, where were ya? I was looking for ya all morning. Did ya check de top toilets?" Mary pointed her mop handle to the ceiling, in the direction of the toilets upstairs.

"Ah, Mam! Dem toilets don't need cleaning."

Veronica knew, that Mary knew that the toilets in this gallery were as sterile as an operating theatre, but Mary knew her job.

"Go up and clean 'em, anyway and make sure everything's there like!"

Veronica clattered off in a huff, dragging her mop behind her.

I remained silent, and Mary continued her dusting, unaware of my observation of her every move. Strange really, that in all the years Mary had spent in and around the gallery, she was totally oblivious to the value, cost or marketing of the art that surrounded her. And yet, in her own uncorrupt way, Mary was an expert in contemporary art. She knew her art; after all, she had seen it all - the Coke tin sculptures, the sand, glass and feather installations, or a man naked except for a bit of toilet paper wrapped around his torso, a turkey leg hanging from his neck.

"Performance?" she muttered as she munched her tea-soaked fig rolls.

"Dat young fella's making a show of himself!"

Yes, she had seen it all over twenty years of cleaning, she knew her art, Mary knew what she liked.

J-Cloth flying, she had completed the full circuit of the gallery, she was heading my direction to collect her mop and brush and move on to the stairs. She looked at me. I felt her gaze was deeper than her own reflection on the glass. I was self conscious. She stopped, stepped back two steps, and stared, and sighed. She then walked right up to me until her nose almost touched the glass.

"Han '95", she whispered the name of my creator, and stepping back again, she panned the whole gallery, the blending of colours, the formation of composition, the intensity, the softness. She stepped forward again.

"Finished de toilets, Mam."

Veronica was back, the bubble burst.

"Good girl," Mary encouraged, Veronica smiled with the embarrassment of pride.

"Isn't dat dotey." Mary pointed at me with the mop. I tensed up, my paint stiffened as I drew back from my mounting in an effort to hold my composition.

"It is, but what is it Mam?" Veronica couldn't make head nor tail of me.

"It doesn't matter what it is!"

Mary drew close to Veronica and went on to explain the unimportance of how a rainbow gets up in the sky, or what makes the sun shine, or where the moon goes by day, or who made the world.

"Dey're all creations," Mary continued.

"And, like all creations, it's a mystery, you either like it or you don't, ... and I like dis."

"It's beautiful, alright," Veronica nodded. She walked back to take in the whole picture.

* * * * *

"Girls!"

I was enjoying the attention, until the curator walked in "Girls!" he repeated, with a tone of authority. "Must get the lead out! Have ye finished the stairs yet?"

"Just starting now, Mr. Peterson." Mary kept her head down.

"Well must get a move on! Big opening tonight!"

Mr. Peterson had a bee in his bonnet.

"Just going now, Mr. Peterson, but ... we were just saying like, isn't dis dotey Mr. Peterson?"

Mary pointed at me.

"Dotey?" he repeated "I don't know if dotey is the correct word to describe this? Have you seen the catalogue?" asked Mr. Peterson.

"Catalogue?" Mary echoed.

"Well if you had seen the catalogue, you would see," he pointed at me, "this described as many things but certainly not 'dotey'. This is a very important piece, a very expensive piece. "

"Worth every penny of it too, no doubt." Mary was indignant. "But I still think it's dotey."

Mary topped her cigarette into her mop bucket, and headed off in the direction of the stairs, giving a brush of her duster to the 'No Smoking' sign, as she trundled off. Mr. Peterson sniffed and held his breath. He placed his hand on my frame, to make sure I hadn't been tampered with. He turned and walked out. The Gallery was lifeless.

II

Flashes from Nikon and Pentax announced the glitterati. Family, friends sponsors, artists, academics, politicians and hangers-on, were well in place. All in all it looked like the makings of a good show. What amazed me was that people spent very little time viewing us and yet, red dots flew up, left and right of me. I was privileged, in that my red dot was in place prior to the exhibition opening proper. Like Gulliver, I towered over these people and yet I was smaller, a 24 x 40 acrylic on paper. I looked at them, and they looked at each other, they were having a ball.

Students searched for culture:

"It's your turn."

"I can't!" came the reply. "Look, I got the last lot."

"I can't just stroll up, and casually pick up six glasses of plonk!" He was under pressure.

"There's a rake a' gargle there. Go on!" he was ordered.

"Jesus, alright, but if I get shagged out," he was protesting.

"Look just get four glasses, two each, and we'll head off for a blast! O.K?" He was convinced.

He struck off, through the furs and silks into the zone where all that glittered was gold. He was as inconspicuous as any eighteen y e a r - o l d art student with a Mohawk and a hacked biker jacket could be, in such a situation. This Mohawk was at a time in his life where he searched for many things from culture to free drink. He returned hands full and smiling, a little boy in a man's frame.

The cultured were present also:
Grey haired suits,
pony tailed sunglasses;
Nodded,
Winked, waved,
shook hands
and generally rubbed shoulders.

Cheque books carried,
Catalogues rolled
and pointed
and slapped against thighs.

They liked what they saw.

* * * * *

Clink! Clink! Clink
"Ladies and Gentlemen, ahem!" Mr. Peterson was buzzing.

An uneasy dash for the last round of gut-rot, freeloaders to the rear and the speeching began. The show was officially opened by the holy trinity of the art world, an academic politician with a high media profile. With a few witty anecdotes, we were all praised, including our creator.

"And now I'd like to declare this Exhibition opened. Thank You!"
They mingled and drank and laughed. This was a good opening.
From the corner of my frame I noticed my creator, he looked stressed. He was cornered by a potential buyer.

"You'd be mad not to accept," argued the buyer.

"I'll pay ya cash, no Gallery fees, what they don't know, won't bother 'em, knock a hundred quid less gallery expenses off, and you'll have an arse pocketful o' cash on your way home..."

"No it must go through the Gallery." The creator backed into the corner.

"What are ya afraid of, you're a fool man!" The buyer pushed.

"Look! I'm not a horse trader, I'm an artist!" The creator was not interested.

"Ah go on ya bluffer, it's my last offer." The buyer made an attempt to walk away, a look of relief came over the creator's face.

"Mr. Hanlon?" a timid voice.

The creator turned. An elegant lady faced him, no furs, no silks, no jewels but nonetheless elegant. From her shoulder length hair held back with a bow, to her slender ankles, this lady oozed elegance.

"Mr. Hanlon?" she repeated.

I nearly jumped off my backing board. It was Mary, Mary the cleaner, in a navy A-line classic and matching petite pumps.

"Don't mind your Mr. Hanlon. Han's the name, everybody calls me Han. What can I do for ya?"

The creator recognized genuine interest.

"I've no invitation," she continued. "I'm the cleaner here, but I felt I just had to come down and tell you that I liked your Art." She was embarrassed.

"Sure, don't I know you?" asked the creator "You've been here for years, since I was a student. You're Mary aren't you?"

"That's right, Mary Harrington," she smiled.

"Well I'm glad you like the show."

"Yeah, it's lovely. In fact that one there" she pointed at me, "I thought that one was really dotey this morning, but this one here," she looked at the painting that had caused the creator such grief with the buyer, "is really cute too."

"Do you really think so?"

The creator looked proud.

"Look!" The buyer was back.

"I'll throw in another fifty quid and that's my final offer!"

The creator whipped a pen from his pocket and printed 'N.F.S.' in broad bold capitals on the white tag under the painting. He placed Mary's arm under his oxter and guided her towards the wine table.

"Would you like a glass a' wine, Mrs. Harrington? Have you seen the rest of the ...?"

They walked off through the masses. Mr. Peterson cleared his throat, sniffed and smiled uneasily. Mary and the creator strolled around the room in conversation, in unison, they chatted and laughed, good belly laughs, totally unaware of the show that surrounded them. He spoke his dreams and ideas, she spoke her observations, simple but no less indepth, accurate and valid. The creator was at home.

The wine ran out, the opening closed, and for the following fortnight, we just hung around. We were observed and analysed, it was nice. It was nice too, seeing Mary and Veronica, their humours and unpredictable routine.

* * * * *

Two weeks had passed, we were manhandled off the wall. I was propped up against a sculpture plinth as my fellow paintings were wrapped and handed over to their respective buyers.

"Are ya sure, ya don't want a hand dere, Mary?"

One of the attendants went to lend a hand, Mary just waved him away.

"Can't you carry on with your own work, I'll look after mine. Thanks anyway."
Mary was busy. She emptied some newspapers and a ball of twine

37

out of a Dunne's Stores bag onto the floor. She proceeded to carefully wrap the painting that lay by my side. Tenderly, she put the parcel back into the bag. Excited, she walked off, with a spring in her step, her treasure clutched, tightly but delicately. The attendants winked, nodded and smiled, she was eager to get home quickly, and unwrap her present.

I too, was wrapped, maybe with not as much care and attention as Mary would have given me, nevertheless the attendants knew their job. I was delivered to the collection of a private collector and placed in a room of my peers, a Louis le Brocquy, a Brian Burke, a Mick Mulcahy.

I have become a point of prestige. It's strange being in this place. I have lost my dream quality, feeling status and inspirational power. I have become a name, in this room of names. I am judged by a language of strict terminology, a language not mine. Life is lifeless, so dull, so sterile.

My creation was my death. I hang here, lifeless. In my happier moments I daydream, how nice just to spend a day over Mary Harrington's fireplace, being loved, being chatted to. But, when I feel low, and, sometimes I get very low, I just wish I had never been created. Before a brush was put to paper, that was the time, before I was hung out to dry. I lived in the mind of my creator, it was a time of eternity, where all was one and yet, none. It was a time of colour and freedom and expression. I could have been expressed as anything, the mystery, the excitement.

We built pyramids and viewed the world through coloured glass.

Arthur, the Exhibitionist and Nigel Rolfe

Coming out of my teens, crossing Patrick's Bridge, I was slap bang in the middle of the Boot Boy era. Twenty-four inch parallels and crombie, hair cropped tightly, snake-eyed, my style was slow and calculating. Evenly paced, air hissed from my punctured Air Wair.

"Hoi Arto ! Arto ! Over Here !"

It was Hacker, Macker and Slasher, weaving between the frustrated, frustrating traffic. Like musketeers, red linings from crombies flashing, and I was D'Artagnan.

They were under pressure.

"Check it out!" Hacker spluttered and pointed in the direction of 5a Bridge Street. I could make out the words, 'TRISKEL ARTS CENTRE' and the word 'EXHIBITION'.

"Dere's a fella' over dere! On his knees, naked!"

Slasher looked shocked.

"A fish tied 'round his neck!"

Macker butted in.

"You're takin' de piss lads?"

I smiled, they did not.

This was something I had to see.

"A bunch a' steamers!" Hacker warned.

We parted company.

It was Voyeuristic!, Masochistic!, Sadistic! 'The Exhibitionist', on his knees and naked, and, like Macker said, a fish tied around his neck. "Somebody pick him up for Christ sake!" my mind screamed, "this man needs help!"

They stood there, sipping wine, mute and pensive, watching. I didn't understand. I was shocked and puzzled, I questioned, maybe I understood. I'm outa' here!

"STEAMERS!" I roared, and scarpered.

Soon after that, me and the Musketeers grew up, signed on

and separated.

* * * *

Ten years squatting in London, I was home for Christmas, looking
for a job.
"Hoi Arto! Over here, Arto!" It was Hacker, it was like I had never
left, gone were the crombies and parallels, but things were the same.
"Of course I'm not workin', I'm an artist," Hacker proclaimed.
"You? You couldn't draw a straight line, maybe you are an artist!" I
slagged. And locking onto his neck, I ran him at the 'Echo boy' outside
Roches Stores, sending Echos flying and earrings jangling as Hacker's
biker jacket crumpled up over his neatly shaven head. Things never
change. That night he brought me to an exhibition opening. We guzzled
free wine, eye-balled women, more drink and on to Zoes for a bop. An
opening addict, that's what I became. Culture, females, Zoes and free
drink, what can I say. Gabba Gabba Hey! It was party time in Artsville
and I was here to stay.

* * * *

"Slasher?" I hesitated. "Slasher?"

I wasn't sure. It must have been twelve years, he was twisted on Liberty
Street, unrecognisable.

"Arto!" He smiled.
I helped him to his feet. We hugged and reminisced, he hadn't seen the
lads for years. I told him I was meeting Hacker. He wasn't interested.
I mentioned an opening and free drink, a fatal mistake. He swayed
there, uninvited and invited himself. What could I say, he was one of
the Musketeers and I was, well, er, only 'De Arto'.

As I carried him down Tobin Street towards the new Triskel Arts
Centre, Slasher cursed and sweared and lashed out at anything that

40

moved, he was crying tears of nostalgia. He was a mess. How would I explain this to Robbie, the curator. I knew that what I was doing was wrong, but when have I ever done the right thing, if given a choice. It was a memorable night, best forgotten.

* * * *

Time flies, things change and people move on. I've moved to the suburbs of Artsville and the manic nights of wine guzzling are gone, gone for me at any rate. I've moved on. I'm not knocking the wine guzzlers, a few glasses of wine is a cheap education. Because, as in my case, eventually the wine guzzler took his eyes off the floor, and looked at the walls. Whatever the reason, it's a good enough reason. It's all exposure.

Exposure? When I think back to that day on Bridge Street, the naked man and fish routine, and how it affected my life. I questioned the medium, the method, the artist, the art. I questioned myself, my being, my perception, my sexuality. Ah yes, my sexuality, I fell in love that day, there I was, a teenager, my first time experiencing nudity and I fell in love with that fish, and to this day I still love fish, and all things fishy.

* * * *

By the way, I heard last week, that poor ol' Slasher was arrested for urinating in a public place, The South Mall. Public place - I ask you? Only a very small elite section of the public have any business being down the South Mall. But anyway, when Slasher was arrested, his only defence was that he was an artist. I could vouch for that, I could stand up in court and swear he was an artist. Slasher was a piss-artist but he was certainly no exhibitionist. Somehow, I don't think that would stand up in court.

Same Old Tune

Nero retched, her hand reached roughly down inside his throat. Bolts of pain shot to his extremities, as her talon-like nails pierced his throbbing heart. She dragged, it pulsating, up past his œsophagus and out through his mouth, blood drenched aorta dangling. She flung it to the floor, stamped on it, spat on it and kicked it across the terraza. He watched as her aerobically taut buttocks swayed across the airport concourse towards the Departures lounge. Nero stood there in his shell-like case, helpless and heart-broken, afraid to turn and walk away. The minutes flashed by on the Departure screen. His eyes begged her not to go but 14:37 became 14:38 and Flight 205 was gone. He went home, turned on the telly, poured himself a bottle of scotch, threw himself down on the couch and watched 'Daithí Lacha'.

Nobody really knew where he got the nickname 'Nero', but it was a name that stuck. A likeable sort of chap, a musician, a quiet and easy- going type, a bit of a dreamer. Sad really, that with all these good traits, that Nero was a misfit. You see, his father abandoned his mother and society abandoned Nero to the status of an illegitimate.

Helena was French. She was young, sensitive and sensual. A quiet sort of girl but this was probably due to the fact that she couldn't understand the Cork accent and her English was shaky at the best of times. She was his Helena, he played the fiddle for her, they loved each other....forever.

With Helena's foreign influence, Nero's horizons were broadened. He no longer had the futile urgency to fit into the society that had pushed him to the fringes. Nero became the 'Continental Paddy'. He ate croissants for breakfast with his sausages, rashers, black and white pudding, eggs and lashings of tea. He could drink pints in the open air as good as the next European, he'd wear shorts from June to September and, at times, he was known to dabble in romance. With Helena leaning on his right shoulder, it somehow balanced the weight of the chip on his left shoulder. Nero was alive and fiddling.

Same Old Tune

It cut him to the bone when she walked out of his life, but she had to get out from under the burden of Nero's problems. While Helena leaned on Nero's shoulder, Nero stood, a dead weight on her mind.
"Kick me in the balls!
Cut off my fiddle fingers!
Anything! Just don't go!"
Nero learned at an early age that feelings hurt, maybe that's why he inevitably substituted pain for feelings.

> *A quiet and easy-going chap.*
> *A likeable sort of guy.*
> *A musician.*
> *A dreamer.*
> *Abandoned.*
> *Again.*

Nero took to drinking; he was always drunk, but he claimed he was sober half of the time. Life crumbled around him, it wasn't that he lost his job, he just chucked it in. Soon his music played second fiddle to drink.

* * * *

The couch was soft and warm. Nero just sat there watching T.V. and sipping scotch. When the scotch ran out, his taste buds became less discerning and, eventually, he drank anything he could get his hands on. A Serpentine Cycle.

SAME OLD TUNE

As he sipped,
he slipped
from steamed
to stoned
and slightly
cynically,
he supped
some more

AND

As she slaved,
she sensed
her self-esteem
slip,
her seduction
sublime,
some steamed
man's whore.

It wasn't that he spent all his time on the couch. He managed to sign on once a week. He got it together to make home-brew and, somewhere along the line, he got married to Mary. They had a clatter of kids. Nero sat there, soft and warm. He watched in a haze as the events of a lifetime flashed by in front of him. In his sober moments his mind threw up images of his drunkenness; he'd cringe.

* * * *

He remembered waking up one morning, lying face down in the front hall, the dog licking the back of his neck. Chips from his batter burger supper were caked into his forehead, as the peas soaked into the camouflaging carpet. His trousers down around his knees, the front door open and his keys still in the lock, he could hear Mary whispering. "Shhhhhh!
Don't be waking your dad!"

The kids tip-toed around him getting ready for school and the dog, finishing the batter burger, started on the peas.

* * * *

There was the time his eldest, Jacinta, got pregnant. It hurt him that she went to the priest before coming to her own father, and then the priest came to Nero. Nero was on his best behaviour. Mary had organised a clean shirt for him and she cleared away the newspapers that always lay around, protecting the couch and carpet where Nero sat. Mary was sick to death of brushing up cigarette butts and the mess that would gather around him. Nero sat there in his clean shirt, the T.V. off, waiting and sober.

Whispers in the front hall announced Father Fitz's arrival. The whispering stopped, the door into the front room swung open.

"Ah, ello Father."

Nero stretched out his hand and made an effort to get out of the couch.

"Stay where you are, Mister Murphy!" Father Fitz smiled.

"Take a seat, take a seat!" Nero pointed.

Father Fitz pulled up a fireside chair. Nero was on his best behaviour. He showed hospitality and all that went with it.

"Will you have a drink, father?"

Father Fitz was caught off guard.

"Eh, maybe...a small one."

Nero needed no more encouragement, he plunged his West Ham United mug into the black plastic, 10 gallon rubbish bin that always stood by the fire, brewing.

"Best home-brew dis side of Texas!"

Nero's eyes sparkled.

Five West Ham mugs later, with the alcohol strength of wine, Nero was only getting into his stride. He had been waiting for a drink since 9 o'clock in the morning and it was now almost noon. Father Fitz was poleaxed. A gibbering mess, he was carried to a waiting taxi. He called around next day to collect his car, and have that chat with Nero, but Nero was asleep.

Same Old Tune

* * * *

Or the time Mary wanted the room painted for Jacinta's wedding, Nero promised he'd organise it. But the wedding drew close and Mary gave up on him. Sean McAuliffe from next door volunteered for the job. Sean covered the furniture with dust sheets, including the couch with Nero, sprawled out on the newspapers, Nero slept through the whole job.

"How de hell did I get here?"

Nero woke around 2:00 a.m. to find the room a different colour, none of the usual photos or plants on the dresser.

"The dresser?" it had moved to the far side of the room.

"No telly? And what's dis? No newspapers!"

In his haze, Nero assumed that he must have somehow strayed into a neighbour's front room. It baffled him as to how he got there in his string vest, underpants and slippers, with no keys! Over the back wall was the only way home.

Mary woke to the sound of Sean McAuliffe banging on the front door, it was nearly 3:00 a.m. Seemingly, Sean had spotted Nero, climbing over the back wall into his garden. Sean assumed Nero was on the war-path, and was coming to do him in. He felt that maybe he had stolen Nero's thunder, by painting the room.

Meanwhile, Nero was just trying to do the right thing, and get home before he was missed.

His memories would have been funny, if they weren't so pathetic. It hurt him. Nero resented the fact that he was a useless father and provider, but what could he do, he was never taught how to be these things. He just drank some more and the pain went away.

II

Nero raised the zapper in his right hand and flicked to RTE 1. Mary ran from the room, in tears. Newspapers crunching, he leaned over the side of the chair, and dunked his mug into the rubbish bin. He needed a drink. Balancing the mug on his left knee, he sat back and closed his eyes.

His peace shattered. The door crashed open.

"Who do you think you are?" It was Imelda, his second oldest.

"Who the hell do you think you are?" she roared, eyeballs bulging.

Nero shook his head.

"A shaggin' maggot, dat's what you are!

A waster,

A useless shaggin' waster."

She was close to tears.

"Hoi!" Nero mumbled.

"Don't talk to your father in dat tone!"

"Father?" Imelda shook with rage.

"Father? You?

You were never a father to me or the rest of us

A! A! Shaggin' excuse for a human being, dat's what you are. Mam just came in here, trying to break the news to you gently so as not to upset ya. And what do ya do? You changed the channel and poured anther drink!"

"What could I do!"

Nero defended.

"You could have shown feelings - sadness!, anger, horror, anything! You, you ... you maggot! Even a maggot has more feelings than ya!"

"It isn't my fault she got cancer!" Nero rationalised.

"You're useless!" Her index finger stretched to within an inch of his nose.

"I hate you. I'm sick of hearing about what a nice guy you were before drink got a hold of ya!

I'm sick of hearing about how good a musician you were!

I'm sick of you!"

Nero puckered his lips and raised an eyebrow.

"Dere was no one wanted for anything in dis house ...

I was always dere for ye!"

His eyes begged sympathy.

"There for us?" Imelda snarled. "Don't make me laugh!
The only reason you were here for us, was because, you were too drunk
to get up out of the couch and be anywhere else. You care about no
one. Not even yourself you're nothing. A shaggin' maggot!"
She stormed out, the door slammed behind her.

Nero stretched his eyelids, and tried to focus, newspapers rustled
like autumn leaves, he felt old. Out between his baldy head and bristled
chin, his eyes twinkled. They rolled down over his chest, a chest any
woman would be proud of, past his beer swollen belly, and onto the
newspaper-covered floor. Slowly he sensed his domain.
"Hhhruuppp!"
He pulled himself up out of the couch, and found his balance. Like a
bear waking from hibernation, he stretched, clenched his eyes shut, and
forced them open again. He rubbed the back of his head, smelled under
his armpits, tugged at his crotch, scratched his arse and farted.
"Good aul'd arse!" He shook himself.
"Jesus!" He put his hands to his ears.
"What's dat godforsaken noise?"
And there was 'Bosco', screaming at him, out of the box.
Nero flicked the off switch and lay the zapper down. He stood there, a
slob in silence.
He heard the tear drops falling, out on the stairs, where Imelda
consoled her mother. Something moved, he stood there motionless.
There's nothing like silence to help a man see.

Slowly he walked to the dresser. Reaching, he fumbled on top, his
fingers disturbing twenty years of dust. He vaguely remembered putting
the fiddle case up there, maybe it was still there? He puffed, and smiled
as the case slipped into his hands, rising a black cloud.
Like a new-born baby he carefully took the fiddle in his arms, and
plucking her untuned stings, he brought her back to life. He stood there,
in his food stained string vest, barefoot on the newspapers, rubbing
resin over the horse hairs, and slowly he drew the bow across the
strings. The strings tingled under his softened fingers, as the notes
vibrated through the sound box into his chest and head, he played, and
slowly it all came back, the pain, the peace, the fighting, the back-biting

and the music became fluid.

He stroked the fiddle. As he concentrated, the music moved through him and the fiddle glowed. Slowly the intensity grew. With that intensity his concentration gave way to his natural rhythms. Nero swayed from side to side, the music filled his head. Newspapers curled and crunched underfoot as he moved, and he played. His breathing was strong and regular as the movement carried him off the newspapers into the war zone; he was Nero. Elbows in the air, head swaying on shoulders, hips twisting, the music moved him around the room, with agility and determination.

Over and over and over again, he played the same tune. It was a tune he had composed for Helena, 'The Humours of Helena', he called it. With each successive playing, his movement and music became freer. Flower pots, photos and ashtrays in the air, Nero moved with intensity around the room. He danced there, barefoot on broken glass, dirt and cigarette butts.

Sliding up the 'E' string he played notes that would have put Jimi Hendrix to shame. His fingers bled. Blood flowed down the neck of the fiddle, and gathered in the palm of his hand, and he played. The bow knocked sparks off the strings, sparks that shot deep into Nero's head and chest, sparks that rekindled a fire, and the intensity grew, and somewhere between the agony and ecstasy, came something he hadn't experienced in a long time; Nero began to feel.

It wasn't that his life flashed before him, well, not like a serialised soap opera, but he sensed his life, a wasted life, the people who loved him, the people who cared, and lived in hope.

He felt no pain from his string-slit fingers, nor the gashes that reddened the newspaper and carpet, as he danced on the glass. But he did feel pain, a deep pain, a pain that had been numbed by drink and depression.

The music surged up inside, as he bounced, pinball-like, from dresser to cabinet. Eyes shut, slowly his cheeks moistened, and the tears fell onto the sound box; the fiddle wailed, ag caoineadh.

SAME OLD TUNE

* * * *

Imelda and Mary sat there on the stairs in each others arms, wet-faced and listening. Nero belted out 'The Humours', to the sound of furniture falling and crashing. Mary was calm, her mind rambled to a time before her life was wasted, to days of hope when she cared, when she loved, but now she felt no pain.
They listened.
"Isn't dat beautiful?" Imelda whispered.
Mary nodded.
"Dat's my tune," her eyes glistened, "he calls it 'Mary's Movement'."
and he played,
and she listened.

Benny was a Daaancer!

"Sure dat's not dancin?"
"RAVE?"
Benny sighed.
"All I want is a dance."
"Sure dat's not dancin'!"
Strange how a happy, crowded room can make a sad heart lonely.

* * * * *

Benny hadn't danced since he was single, real dancing. He'd freak out for the fast set, like Rory Gallagher, with his imaginary guitar, right hand hitting those difficult notes down as far as his knee. Then the slow ones, three clingers, locking onto any girl who'd let him. He'd stand there rubbing his teenage hands up and down her back, up and down her tight lambswool crewneck, hoping for a feel of bra strap. Real dancin' and then, in for the kill, eyes shut, tongue back the throat and suck face. Up and down went the hands, three more fast ones. He'd stand there for half the first song, clung on, then disengage and straight back to the imaginary guitar of the Status Quo.

* * * * *

The place was alive with Ravers, eyes popping, hands, feet and knees looping, bodies contorted. They were ecstatic.
"I'll never get the hang a' dis." Benny was low.
He plonked his three quarter empty pint of Murphy's on the juice bar, turned and walked out. It was a cold walk home and a colder home ahead of him now that Mary was gone. She was gone with the kids, she was gone for good.
"So much for 'for better or for worse'!"
Benny clipped an empty beer can, sending it clattering across the road.

BENNY WAS A DAAANCER!

"'Tis true what they say 'bout empty cans!" Benny thought to himself and he headed up the hill homeward, towards the North Infirmary.

* * * * *

Ah yes! His first dance, Cork Con., nicely steamed, one eighth of a bottle of Vodka inside him. Barely a boy and he was out looking for a woman. They stood there in the corner, being foolish, observing the big bucks. His courage fading, Benny knew it was now or never.

"They shoot horses, don't they?"

cackled from the battered speakers.
Benny made his move. He eased onto the dance floor, mouse-ish.
"Are ya dancin'?" He tapped her shoulder.
"What's it look like, fatso!" She smiled, exposing a mouth like Barrack Street, where every second tooth was battered, broken or demolished. Benny assumed she was, so he grabbed onto her, his first clinger. A new experience. And then it happened, a most excruciating pain in the place where you don't put food. A size 10 Doc Marten lifted him off the floor, the jealous boyfriend syndrome. Benny had a lot to learn, but weeks passed, he learned the steps of courtship, and Benny was a Dancer.

* * * * *

The front door creaked open to a smell of death and decay. Benny had missed the rubbish collection again, and, since Mary left, he had systematically worked his way through every cup, saucer and plate in the house, and now he was munching directly from tin or packet.
Every room was a dining room, even the toilet had two empty cereal bowls and a clatter of cups. His castle in tatters, the kingdom destroyed, Benny needed a Queen.
"I'll have to learn to Rave," he figured it out!
Friday; Benny was back among the Ravers. Ten pints into the night, his ankles loosened. Sports coat bulging under his 40-inch-waist Farah

trousers, his steps clumsy. He was over dressed and over nourished. He looked hick, but he was Raving, raving from drink.

"Techno! ..Techno! ..Techno!" the sounds buzzed.

Benny moved cautiously, under the gaze of a thousand dilated pupils, he was there to learn. The girls danced with the girls and the boys danced with the boys, with no physical contact, no conversation, no slow ones. But Benny was dancing, and for the first time in his life, dancing for dancing's sake, and loving it.

"Benny the Raver." Big Daddy of the Rave Scene. They liked him, they stepped aside and made room, not only because of his clumsiness, but also out of respect, respect for a trier. The weeks were good to Benny, and Benny, 'King of the Ravers', raved on! A King without a Queen, but it didn't matter, he had a life, he lived for Friday nights; Benny was a Raver!

* * * * *

She was beautiful, a little older than the rest, not so wild, not so whackerish. She raved there every week, over by the fire exit. Benny had noticed her;

"Hop to the left...two, three

Hop to the right....two, three," he concentrated.

'E' pumping through him, sweat bubbling from his nose, neck, knees and armpits, he was as fresh as a daisy.

"Close the eyes ..two, three

shake the hips....two, three..!" He mouthed his well-rehearsed steps, steps practised at home to his 'River of Rave' compilation tape, steps well practised, but rigid.

"Pump it up Pu Pu Pu Pu!

Pump it up"

Benny opened his eye. There she was. It was like she was dancing for him and him alone.

Legs wide open, head down, hair over her face, her hands waved and weaved in and out between her knees. Bending under flexing thighs, she leaned back as far as gravity would allow, hands rolling up past her well-formed, silhouetted body.

" Pu, Pu, Pu, Pu, Pump it up!"

She surged no more than two feet from Benny's bulging belly. He mimicked her movement, not with perfection, but as best he could.

"My Queen, two three."

It dawned on him,

"My Princess, two, three.

Hop to the right, two, three.

Must impress, two, three.

Try a new step, two, three."

Benny diverged from his well-rehearsed routine into a series of furious scissor kicks; this was his chance.

Hands flying faster and faster, ravers stopped, stepped back and stared, wondering 'what the hell is he on?'

Faster and faster into open space, eyes shut, Benny's legs flew in and out, he had an audience. This was it. Now was the time. His eighteen-stone bulk bounded across the floor and with a hop, skip and a most almighty jump, Benny was airborne.

Suspended there in mid air for what seemed like an eternity, intending to hit the floor, heel to toe and into the splits, he hung there.

"This is it!

This is Uh! Uh! Uh! Uh!"

It was like a vice grips crushing his rib cage. Everything was blue and hazy. He crashed gracelessly in a heap to the floor, bursting his skull wide open as it hopped from table to step to floor.

"Mind his head!

Give him room, for Christ's sakes!"

She leaned over him, unbuttoning his shirt.

"You're O.K.! I'm a nurse.

Do you know who you are?" She rubbed his chest.

Benny's eyes rolled in his head.

"I think it's his heart!" she whispered.

"Call an ambulance."

"Who am I?" Benny mumbled.

"I'm Benny. I'm a Daaancer!"

BENNY WAS A DAAANCER!

His pupils rolled one more time, and his eye lids closed to whiteness, he saw Mary and the kids, and the good old days.
"Wha' did 'e say?"
"I think he said he was a dinosaur?"
Out of time and out of place...
Benny was a Dinosaur!

Rites of Passage

"**J**ojo flaked him in between the eyes, and roared, 'you've no rights to pass through here.' The Guard picked himself up and scarpered. A hard man boi ... Jojo was a hard man!"

He cackled, exposing gums as tough as ivory.
Eyes sparkling, his mind turned the pages. I sat there driving, hungover and late for work.

* * * *

It was Saturday morning. I was supposed to be in for ten, and I had been out 'til three the night before. My beer-floating cranium was rattled by an early morning phone call. Head splitting, tongue furry, small talk didn't come easily.
"Course I'll drive ya, Dad." It's hard to refuse a man who never said no.
"I'll be there in a minute," I reassured.
All I wanted to do was put down the receiver and drink my Solpadeine but he wanted to talk.
"They're falling like flies around me!" he explained.
This was his fourth funeral in almost as many weeks, a tight schedule in an otherwise slack social events calender.
"Listen Dad, me head is burstin' open, put down the phone and I'll be up to ya as soon as I can," I begged.
"Just drop me out to Jojo Duggan's House," he bargained "He'll drive me to the funeral. A hard man is Jojo." He was ready to settle in for a long chat.
"Good bye!" I said, and hung up.
Jojo Duggan. Now there was a name that echoed around our house over the years.
Jojo was a man that myths were made of. He fought in the war, but nobody was really sure which war he fought in, he was supposed to

have been in jail, or on the run, or something; myth-making defies definition.

I had heard all the stories, blow by blow, tear by tear, and yet I never actually met Jojo. I suspected that maybe my mother had barred him from our house, because, myths or no myths, Jojo was a hard man, and my father, well, I was a married man.

I dragged myself out of the bed, performed the necessary and drove to the collection point. He was at the door, cap on head.

"Hop in Dad, I'm mad late."

He sat in, and it started. It was Jojo this and Jojo that.

"Do I know Jojo?" I interrupted.

"Everybody knows Jojo!" he replied and carried on.

The Solpadeine was beginning to work on the drink damage, and my head was cloudy from the effects of it. I have never had respect for drunken drivers, and there I was, way over the limit, my only defence was that I wouldn't be doing it if I was sober. I sat there steamed, stuck in traffic, late, with no self respect. He churned it out, pausing occasionally to give directions, take a breath or swallow spit. I was not entertained, but his stories filled my head, despite myself.

Jojo was larger than life, feared by his enemies, treasured as a friend and loved by all women.

"... and then! Jojo picked up the bicycle, swung it over his head, and threw it. Well! It flew through the air knocking four of the Kenmare lads. I pounced on two of them while Jojo sorted out the other six. They ran for their lives ... tough as nails boi." His boyish eyes sparkled inside their well-worn sockets.

"Do you know Jojo long?" My interest was roused.

"The best a' buddies, inseparable ! We came to Cork together. We worked in Ford's together"

Enough background information, he was off on another story. As the stories flowed, I listened and there in front of me, magically, a picture of Jojo was conjured up from a sea of words. He was invincible, in sport and in war, always one to fall in if there was a job to be done, the first to volunteer.

Rites of Passage

"... so ...
Jojo unharnessed the dead horse,
and got under the cart himself
pulled it, all the way to the creamery,
a horse of a man, was Jojo!"
He thumped the dashboard with a laugh.
"A horse of a man." he repeated.
"Do I go left or right here, Dad?" I begged direction.
"Straight on!" he roared and the stories continued.
"And the day we cycled to Innishannon, drank two quarts, ran in the sports. Jojo came first, I came second. More drink ... cycled to Kenmare ... more drink. A dance, some courtin', fought five townies and won! And cycled home in time for work next morning! And that was a quiet night!" He smiled defiantly.
The stories smelt of embellishment, but the exaggeration was always within the limits of credibility, making it next to impossible to know where facts faded and fiction fostered.
"Slow down!" his hand stretched out "This is it. Park behind the red Fiesta!"
I pulled in.
"Will ya come in and say hello to Jojo?" he enquired.
"I'm mad late Dad! Make sure it's the right house before I head off!" I advised.
He pulled himself out of the passenger seat and vanished in the garden gate. I changed channel on the radio, trying to find the right time. Looking up, he was back at the gate, beaming! Mission accomplished, I started the car.
"Hoi ... Wait!" he shouted.
"Jojo's comin' out to see ya ... wait one sec." his eyes pleaded.
I threw my eyes to Heaven, and prayed. He stood down from the path and stepped to one side. There stood Jojo.
A sharp intake of breath, I stared. My day dreams shattered, and I stared. He was old. Old, crumpled and grey, nose runny, eyes watery and skin about three sizes too big for him. My father stood flanking Jojo, smiling from ear to ear. His smiles were genuine, smiles of pride.

He was with Jojo, Jojo the invincible.

Try as I might, I could see no more than my eyes would reveal. He was an old man, a vulnerable old man. Jojo hobbled around to the driver's side, lowering the window, I clasped his shaking hand, steadying it.

"De last time I saw you, you were only a little child."

There was fire in his eyes.

"Will ya come in for a cup?" He sniffled.

(It's amazing the effect that two Solpadeine down on top of a feed of drink has, it's a cocktail that sorts out the head but destroys the brain. Because at that moment, a very profound thought occurred to me, but I can't remember exactly what it was. It ran along the lines of... if I was a child when Jojo last saw me, he must have been in his prime then, and I must have been the small vulnerable one.)

"Sure any son of this man here," Jojo pointed to my father, "has no right to pass Jojo Duggan's house without calling in for a cup." His eyes steadied under shaking brow.

"Well, if I've no right to pass, I'd better come in! I heard what you did to the Guard!" I winked.

He left a roar of a laugh out of him and wheezed, and coughed, and spluttered and coughed, and laughed.

* * * *

The cough bottle was placed on the table "Cough bottle?" I questioned, and three crystal clear cups were poured.

"Down, the course cut, boi! That'll soften your cough!" Jo Jo laughed.

"All the way from the hills of Macroom, the best you'll get!"

The feeling was warm, and we drank to the dead.

They never made it to the funeral that day, and I never made it to work. We raised our cups to the health of the dead over and over again. These men knew death, they laughed at death, they had fought death many times, and won.

He Ain't Heavy

Hairs stiffening to a ridge along the back of my neck like a trapped animal, teeth grinding and knuckles whitened, frightened.

> *I'll kill him*
> *Maybe he hasn't seen me?*
> *Bastard!*
> *I'll kill him,*
> *Maybe he won't recognise me.*

* * * *

A sleepy Sunday morning on Half Moon Street, and just around the corner - Christmas. I was walking off a bit of self-inflicted pain. You know how sometimes, after a skinful, the hangover can be pleasurable, if you've the time or the inclination to go with the flow. Well that's how it was.

Three days on the rip, a bit burned out, nerve endings frayed, throat and nose blocked with the fags but, all in all, I was feeling fine and enjoying my lobotomised stroll through the streets 'til the pubs opened, and then back in for the cure.

I found myself on Paul Street, when fate took a hand to my feet, and turned them into French Church Street. My head was bells and seagulls and pigeons and footsteps and a kango hammer right between my eyes.

> *Footsteps?*
> *Faint footsteps?*
> *On French Church Street?*
> *Far, far from me.*
> *And me?*
> *Far, far from home.*

He Ain't Heavy

And there he was, in black, in the distance. The bastard who tormented and tortured me and my brothers when we were too young to defend ourselves. Brother Keenan. I couldn't see his face. 'Twas his walk I recognised.

He shuffled along French Church Street in my direction. I was trapped, no way out. My only escape was an about face. But I had lost face to that man once too often in the past. So a course was set for a head-on collision.

The shine of his Brylcream, swish of his soutane, smell of the chalk dust were the sights, sounds and scents that haunted my life. I'd wake up some mornings in a bath of sweat. "Thank Christ I've no school anymore!" It wasn't so much the pain from the leather, it was in the anticipation that the terror lay.

I'll kill that bastard...

The things I wouldn't do to that man if I ever came face to face with him had echoed from bar stool to home and back. I had vowed it many times in the past, publicly, usually in a public house in a bout of drunken bravado and here I was, trapped by my own pride.

Bastard!

A coherent word ran through my brain. My pocketed fist clenched tightly as I remembered the wind-whistling leather, sometimes systematic, sometimes sporadic and, like a wolf with a herd of sheep, he'd swoop, pick the most vulnerable and destroy. The sheep huddled closer in silence.

* * * *

Seánie Cronin, young Seánie...

His dad hadn't worked in years, I suppose for the best part of young Seánie's short life. Ma Cronin's nerves were bad, she had taken to the bed and, probably because he had so much time on his hands, Da

Cronin took to porter. Anyway, the upshot of the whole shebang was that young Seánie was always late for school, well, half of the time anyway.

> "The clock was stopped, Brother."

A good excuse for a 10-year old, a feeble excuse for a Christian Brother.

> "'Twas stopped then,
> was it Seánín."

Brother Keenan smiled as he grabbed Seánie by the ears, lifting him clean off the floor and swinging him in the direction of the window.

> "Can ya see the clock on Shandon,
> Seánín?"

Seánie squealed, Brother Keenan smiled and the sheep, giggling nervously, huddled.

* * * *

My pace was slow, his face out of focus. One quick clatter into the ear, my assault plan formulated.

* * * *

Jimmy Murphy...Murph.
Murph's Mam and Dad fought like cat and dog, we all knew it, but there was no shame in it. They loved each other, that was how they got on. Murph would be up half the night listening to this carry-on down in the kitchen, there was no real harm in it, but it must have been hard to sleep through. So, 'twas no wonder that, one Monday morning, small Murph was keeled over, head down on the desk, asleep.
Like a soaring vulture, Brother Keenan's hand cast a shadow over the

back of Murph's bowl-cut poll and, with a roar of "Wake up Man!", his manly hand crushed a clatter across small Murph's ear, a clatter that lifted him out of his desk and up against the wall in a heap, under the shadow of the Virgin.

"You look more comfortable there, Man!
You can stay there."

The sheep closed ranks and Murph remained where he was, kneeling by his desk for the rest of that day.

* * * *

Bastard!

My mind screamed. My right hand slipped from my pocket in preparation for the retribution, his cold eyes pierced the bridge of my nose.

"Ó Murchú," his cheeks stretched to a smile, a smile I had learned to fear but, in a strange sort of way, I was flattered. Brother Keenan must have had more than 2,000 boys at the end of his leather and, here, on French Church Street, after twenty five years, he recognised me.

"Ciarán Ó Murchú, nach éa?"

He thought I was my older brother Ciarán.

Ní hea, a bhráthair, ach Seán," I explained.
"Ah, conas tá tú, a Sheáin?"

How are ya Seán? How are ya indeed.
Why am I speaking Irish to this tyrant?
It's the language he terrorised me with.
His language.

HE AIN'T HEAVY

My mind was travelling at a fierce speed.

I raised my elbow, ready to shoot out one clean smack into his ear, just as he'd draw alongside, but once again, he out manoeuvred me and stopped. Being caught off guard, I stopped too and answered him. A reflex reaction.

"I'm fine, Brother,
How's yourself?"

And then he started.

"Ah sure,
I'm retired now,
I miss de old days,
I miss de boys,
The good old days."

Goodolddays, my mind reeled,
Goodolddays me arse.

And without taking a breath, he continued.

"Yourself, Ciarán and Padraig got on famously...
God bless ye,
I always knew ye would," he smiled.

My big fist tightened, so tight it burned. I remembered a time when that fist wasn't big enough to conceal a gobstopper. That little fist burned too, six lashes of a leather, the Christian was teaching me a lesson, it was for my own good I was reassured but, for the life of me, I can't remember my crime.

Brother Keenan stood there, rambling on about the 'Good Ol' Days', watery eyes rolling between wrinkled lids. He talked of my brothers, Ciarán and Paddy, their wives, their children, their lives, the detail was frightening.

My eyes skimmed across the top of his brush cut, a view I'd never seen in the 'Good Ol' Days'. He must have shrunk, or maybe I had... (Ah forget it!)

He didn't seem menacing, his collar was looser, his brush cut grey and less defined. He mentioned boys' names, names I couldn't remember. He talked of the hurling and football greats, and, beaming with pride, a fatherly pride, his mind filed through the pages of the lives of politicians, businessmen and statesmen. 'My lads', he called them, and he stood there smiling. And then, he talked of the social changes, the modern world, vandalism, crime and violence.

> "Different days, ha!" he threw his eyes to God.
> "No controllin' them these days.
> What these young gurriers need is a good clip in the ear,
> and that would sort 'em out" he swallowed spit.

Enough of this gibberish, the time for talking was over, but then I said something.

> "Brother!
> Dere's a few fellas around,
> Who wouldn't mind giving
> you a flake into the ear," my dander up, my fist knotted.

Brother Keenan smiled. His eyes softened.

> "Sure what young fella
> didn't fall out with his father?
> I always had my lads' best interest at heart."

And, in his own strange way, he was making sense.

He Ain't Heavy

"Ya see," he continued.
"My calling was to help young fellas,
Poor young fellas,
Young fellas like meself," and once again he smiled.
"Did you know," he looked through me,
"I'm a bastard ..."

"Ya serious?" This was no news to me.

"Or, what is it now." he continued.
"Illegitimate is it?
My father ran off before I was born,
The Brothers are my family.
And the boys?
They're my lads," and he smiled again.

And for the first time, his terrorising smile became a smile of pain,
Brother Keenan's pain.

"Ye were all great lads,
And I think of ye,
All the time."

His lips tightened and he went to pass by. My fist contorted and just as
he drew level;

"Brother Keenan?" my right elbow rose to shoulder
height.

"Seán?" he hesitated.

Right hand dipped.

"Happy Christmas, Brother Keenan." We shook
hands.

He Ain't Heavy

"Nollaig fe Mháise duit!" he smiled.

My grip relaxed on his soft chalky fingers and he shuffled off.
My hand regnarled into a knotted fist and I smashed it down into my
left palm. After a lifetime of emotional self-mutilation, there I was on
French Church Street actually physically hitting myself. I was a mess. I
had just missed my once in a lifetime opportunity to even all the odds.

> *Let him off*
> *Go after him.*
> *One flake into the head.*
> *No!*

I watched as that distinctive shuffle faded off into the loneliness, back to
his own hell, or heaven, I'd never know.
Brother Keenan turned into Paul Street, and walked out of my life.

* * * *

It was a sleepy Sunday morning on French Church Street and, just
around the corner, Christmas. I was walking off a bit of self-inflicted
pain, you know how it is? But fate took a hand to my feet and I
stopped, I didn't go for that drink, the violence was over, the cure had
set in. So, I went home to my wife and children, first time in three days.

The Entomologist

His face was kicked in, he was crossing the bridge by the Opera House and heading in our direction.

* * * *

I was standing outside the gallery with a friend of a friend, being told the importance of having a working knowledge of conversational French, if I were to get a job in Euro Disney.

"Plenty of work there, sanitary and maintenance, that sort a' thing," I was informed.

"Did you get to meet le Mickey Mouse?" Cool question I thought.

"I'm sick to death of that crack since I came home from Euro!" A cooler reply.

It was late Saturday afternoon and the streets were thronged, bumper to bumper, nose to tail, like ants. If you've ever lifted a stone off an ant-hive, you'll know what I mean. People were walking over each other with a sort of ant-like predetermination: No stop, no chat, no nod, no wink, heads down and scurrying.

So there I was talking about Mickey Mouse to a pseudo-academic intellectual, ten years my junior, a guy I hardly knew, and him telling me that I'd be better off getting a job as a rubbish collector in Disneyland. The town was crawling, and out of the corner of my eye, I couldn't help but notice the guy with the kicked-in face. He was lean and mean, still on course, coming our way.

As the mangled face came closer, it struck me that this face was a face from my past. I couldn't actually put a name, time or place on this face, and then it came to me. His name was John, John something or other, we sat in the same desk in school, from babies to first class, he was my first friend. Coming face to face with one of my earliest memories was a bit of a blow for the nostalgia banks.

At this stage, my francophone friend of a friend was talking about the cost of Parisian accommodation.

"Well, a garret flat, you couldn't swing a cat in, would cost you," he stretched his hands out to show me the size.

"Actually, it's hard to give an exact cost, because obviously it depends on where the apartment is situated."

This educated Euro-traveller was not very enlightening.

"But you can be sure it would cost a lot more than a flat here," he continued.

I wasn't going to let him off the hook so easily.

"So what you're trying to say is, that an inexpensive flat in Paris would cost you as much as an expensive flat here?" I asked, showing unprecedented interest.

"Yeah," came a pensive reply.

"So, what would an expensive flat in Paris cost?" I probed.

"Jesus! I don't know, but it would cost a lot more than an expensive flat here."

Enough said about accommodation, he was now talking about the night life around Euro Disney. I had visions of hundreds of young, educated, French-speaking, Irish rubbish collectors, blowing referees' whistles with Mickey Mouse ears on their heads, raving the night away on 'E', man. It certainly sounded different.

I found it difficult to keep eye contact with my Europhile friend as my eyes and mind were drawn over his right shoulder, to John, my friend with the mashed face, who at this stage was no more than twenty yards from us. He was smiling but as my eyes focused, it became clear that his smile was more of a permanent feature, a knife gash which ran from the corner of his lip to his right ear lobe. He was my partner in school. I remembered holding hands as we lined up in pairs in the yard. September winds would curl around our dirty, exposed knees and we'd stand there, lined up, holding hands, feeling the cold and fearing the classroom. Me and my partner used to eat our lón in the corner of the shed furthest from the toilets. Jam sandwiches and a ponnie of milk, maybe a lemon bun from the teacher, Miss...Miss...Miss Reynolds. Jesus, it was all coming back! The memories were irregular and inconsistent, probably due to the fact that I was only four or five years of age when these all important memories were being formed. I had memories of short pants, a dog named Trixi and "O Angel of God! My Guardian Dear." I couldn't remember any major conversations we ever had, but then again, what do kids of that age talk about.

I remembered a grey/blue balaclava that Johnny's granny knitted for him (it buttoned under his chin). It looked so snug inside the hood of his duffel coat, I always wanted a balaclava, like Johnny's but my granny was dead. Like all kids of the same age, there was an ongoing superiority conflict between us, but deep down, I knew I held a trump card, you see, his father was only a bus conductor, mine was a bus driver.

So there I was, with my educated Euro-Rubbish Collector, he was talking about the traffic in Paris.

"Cata-feckin'-strophic!
the only word for it...
They drive like looneys."

Once again, his hands in the air, in a very Mediterranean fashion, he was making a point and making it forcefully, so forcefully, in fact, that the shoppers who didn't duck, bounced.

"And, what kind of car are you driving...?
...Citröen?...Renault?" I asked.

"Car?..." his voice raised in pitch.

"I've no car, sure I can't even drive."

"Is this man for real?" I thought to myself.

"I'm just telling you how the French drive..." he continued.

"...Bloody looneys, the whole lot of them...
It's a wild, a crazy place, Man!"

His hands were stretched out like King Canute, trying to stop waves of laden-down shoppers. He babbled on about the cost of car insurance and road tax, this traveller was making no sense.

John was now only a few feet away, his notched face became clearer and the successive layers of nicks and splits were well concealed by a bruising he had obviously received recently. It was this latest addition which made his face look so hideous. His eye was badly swollen, where the white was a blood red and his cheek and forehead were scraped, bruised and battered, his lower lip was split, and yet, he walked with confidence, chin out on hunched shoulders and, by his side, keeping pace, his shorter and less bruised side-kick. John seemed proud of his battle scars as he strode along with a gaatch of authority. The last time I had seen John, the both of us were wearing white bánín suits, and were walking around the North Cathedral, me and my partner, we were on our way to becoming strong and perfect Christians, same school, different class. He had grown up strong alright, but he was far from perfect. John was tough and mean and Christian by birth. The seemingly oblivious masses automatically parted and made way for John and his buddy, they passed by, unhindered, unacknowledged.

It was clear to me that John had noticed my scrutinising gaze, since I clapped eyes on him crossing the bridge. What was not so clear was whether he remembered those cold schoolyard days in short pants, maybe he didn't carry memories, or, maybe it wasn't as I remembered, or maybe...

Hands were flying in the air as my travelled friend chuntered on about women, money and the price of drink. By this stage, John and his right-hand man, had drawn level to us. I raised an eyebrow and threw a nod of recognition at him. He turned his head in my direction, and winked his good eye. Without missing a beat of the pavement or upsetting the swaying of shoulders, they paced by.

"Man! Oh man!,
Did ya see your man's face?
...Dodgy boi...!" observed the Rubbish Collector.

I just nodded. I didn't fear John's scarred face, it was the man who put the scars there I feared. In fact, something inside me wanted to reach out to John,...but to what end? John and his buddy, like Don Quixote and Sancho Panza, ploughed on through the citizens, regardless. I was that boy's partner, we held hands.

"Well, I'm just going in here for a croissant and coffee,
...will ya join me?,
...I'll fill ya in on Disney!" an invitation from the Marco Polo of rubbish men.

I looked at the perfect, sallow complexion of my travelled friend of a friend, his healthy hair, bright eyes and sparkling teeth, he smiled. Through his smile, I saw confusion, disillusion...neglect. I could see my reflection in his pupils, he looked at me.

It occurred to me that we all carried scars, but John carried his well. Most scars heal with time, while others are best covered up and forgotten. I could see the regular bobbing of John's head fade off into the distance, into the haze of aimless shoppers, a grasshopper in a nest of ants.

* * * *

Incidentally, the coffee was delicious, a good Nicaraguan, organic, freshly ground. The croissant, well, it was so-so, or so I was informed.
"Not quite as good as one would get in a patisserie,
on a side street of Paris.
All in all, not bad for Cork, though."
There were a few grasshoppers on the ant hive that day. At least, two or three that I knew of.

Penny For Your Thoughts

With only an ear, a few toe-nails and a bit of a jaw bone left on the plate, I sucked the last bit of salt from some gristly splinters of wrist bones. Wiping my hands along my trousers, I spat the bones and gristle out, out on top of what was once a smiling pig's head. Raising the glass to my lips I could feel the bitter-sweet Murphy's cut through and wash down the greasy salt bacon.

"Ah! heaven."

My left hand stretched out for a Major.

Through the ass of the frothy porter-stained glass, I could see the outline of the bottles, optics and assorted bar implements on their different shelves, lined up behind the counter. These shapes, when seen through the smoke that just hung there in the darkness, lit up by the odd shaft of cold shining sunlight, sparked a memory, an old memory.

* * * *

The homes on the headland slept peacefully as that March sun cut along the deck of the 'Duke of Rothersby'. The holy ground, though almost within an arm's reach seemed so far away that morning, as we glided along the rippled surface of Rosslare Harbour. I felt like jumping overboard, clothes an' all, and swimming ashore. Better sense kept me on the right side of portside. I had a bellyfull of McArdles the previous night and there was no talking to it. It was only a matter of time or luck whether that belly of beer would jump overboard or stay uneasily where it was, swishing from side to side with every gentle roll of the keel.

Big heads with red faces, hairy noses and ears, and mad blood-shot eyes, surfaced onto the deck. Voices, rough from cigarette smoke and cackling laughs from drink, broke the numb silence.

"Yerah! how're ya today, Con?"

"Wrecked boi, me v'ice is knackered."

Beer bottles, bodies and butts were littered between decks, as I made my way below for a cup a' tea to settle the stomach and fill those stretched and seemingly unending minutes until docking time. I was feeling good, with my own people, going home.

The 'Auld Duke' was our Moses and the beer bottles gave us our heavenly Manna. We were, for the most part, the men who built London and other major English cities, we built the subways, motorways and flyovers. We were the men who felt alienated by a culture so overwhelmingly similar to our own, that we became strangers on our own door-step. We were 'Paddies', we were 'McAlpines', we were 'Molly Maguires'. We were never to be British and, in being ourselves in the pubs around Kilburn and other such places, we were typical Irishmen, a type that can only be found in immigrant bars, but never on the auld sod.

Finding myself on the curved platform of Kent Station in Cork at about half past nine, I turned to Mick who, as luck would have it, happened to be still by my side. He cut the travel time from Rosslare to Cork in half by sharing the journey. Intending to say,
"Good-bye and Good luck!"
when I opened my mouth the words I heard were;
"Will ya have a pint?"
"Ah sure, I'll have a straightener before I strike west."
Mick smiled and we crossed the road to the 'Park View'.
Tapping on the window, I shouted in a whispering voice through the letterbox.
"Mary! Mary! come down and let us in."
With a nod and a wink we shuffled from foot to foot. The sound of bolts sliding with keys and chains rattling could be heard from the far side of the door. As the door opened we could hear John cursing under his breath. His sleepy, grumpy head pivoted upwards until his eyes came level with my chin, his lips broadened.
"Well, Christ, Con, come in,
come in,
Well! Well! if it isn't yourself now
Come in, come in!"
He locked the door behind us and poured two creamy pints of

Murphy's. The conversation flowed as the pints poured. I was sad to hear of Mary's death, but I was feeling too good to be getting involved in John's sense of loss. Sure wasn't I on me holidays.

With a nod and a wave, John made his way out from behind the bar and up the lonely stairs. In an effort to milk our mutual company, Mick and myself retreated from our bar stools to the sanctuary table in the corner. There was talk of women, and the price of the pint, the G.A.A. and a bit of politics. We reminisced on the bitter-sweet memories of lonely drunken nights in Kilburn. At about midday Mick picked up his bag and with a shout of,

"Up the Republic!"

he was gone. There he was, like the real John Wayne, heading out to the wild west of Ireland, to return to the city at a future date, shovel for hire.

I found myself alone, and my mind drifted. It was good to be home, amongst friends, drinking Murphy's, smoking Major and spending Irish money. I was steamed and my thoughts were pleasant and varied. I took a handful of coins from my pocket and after they fell from my hardened hand to the table; I lined them up, harps up. One of the pennies had a Queen's head on it. I pushed the coins around the table, making shapes and trains and snakes.

It was nice to see the Irish coins again. These coins could only be used in slot machines in England, shops and pubs wouldn't accept the coins with the harp. I turned them over, appreciating every stroke of Celtic craftsmanship. I fondled them and caressed them. On the ha'penny I could see the sow with her bonhams, it reminded me of a picture I had once seen in an old *Punch* magazine. It was a picture of an Irishman with a big red head and tufts of hair sticking out from under his hat, nose and ears. He had a rope tied around a pig's neck and the caption read:

"A PIG GOING TO MARKET."

The memory insulted me. In a fit of drunken nationalism, I shouted
"Animals!
do ya hear me?

dey treat us like animals.
We're like the dirt we dig.
Never again boi.
You mark my words.
Never again..."

Muttering and cursing to myself, I continued to turn the coins one by one. There in front of me lay the whole menagerie of Irish L.S.D. There was the hen with her chickens on the penny and the rabbit on the tru'penny bit, the sixpence had the greyhound, the bull on the shilling, the two shilling piece with the salmon and the half-crown with the horse.

My attention turned to the penny with the Queen's head.

"A kangaroo? A bloody kangaroo." I laughed.

An Australian penny slipped to me one night about six months previously. It has followed me around from pocket to pocket and pub to pub ever since. A useless piece of copper, but impossible to throw away.

I sat back and smiled. This kangaroo, an animal I knew nothing about, threw a different light on the pig of our ha'penny. The sight of the pig didn't seem to insult me as much as previously, after all, there are two sides to every coin. I remembered hearing somewhere that the pig was one of the most intelligent animals. My mind's eye studied each animal as they lay there on the table.

The Hen with her chicks became Mother Ireland, nurturing, protecting and feeding the weakest. The Rabbit, a symbol of fertility and the large families of the predominantly Catholic nation of celts that lived on this island. The Greyhound brought visions of Cú Chullain and the swiftness of the Fianna of ancient times and how they preserved our nation physically and morally. The strength and temper of the Bull, an animal to be feared when provoked, like Irish manhood over the centuries. The knowledge that was given to our nation by the Salmon of Knowledge through Fionn MacCumhaill could be seen in the two shilling piece. While the horse depicted the force and endurance of the Irish people which came to the fore in successive famines, rebellions and persecutions. I sat back contented and relieved, but all that was an old memory.

Penny For Your Thoughts

II

My once hardened hand lowered the near empty glass from my face. With the obscurity of the frothy glass removed from in front of my eyes, the bottles and optics behind the counter no longer had the appearance of houses on a headland. With a slight thud, a pint of stout was placed in front of me by a familiar old hand.

"How did ya find the pig's head and crubeens?" John asked.

"Pig's head?" I mumbled.

He looked down at the devoured mass on the plate.

"Are ya finished it? Will I take it away?" he went on.

I pointed to some coins on the table.

"You can, take it out a' that, dere, John."

He raised his leg, placed his foot on the stool next to me, bent over and counted the money into his hand.

"10, 20, 30, 40, and 5 and 3.

That will be one pound and 48 new P, Con. Thanks."

He raised this head sideways and looked at me.

"You never went back to England that time, Con, did ya?"

I looked up at his old face. He continued.

"You must be back now, almost 20 years?"

"Eighteen and a half," says I.

I looked down at the Harp on the half new pence, it was smaller and shinier. Turning it, I could see a Celtic design of a sort of a bird. On closer inspection it didn't look anything like any bird I had ever seen. The bird depicted was weak-necked and gangly. It was twisted and contorted and its head shoved up its rear-end.

Decimalisation was here, and here to stay. And, it seemed to me that we were all too busy fiddling with our metric conversion tables to heed the announcements of the changes yet to come. We were being transformed into a flock of weak-necked birds that view the world with heads twisted between our legs and up our collective arse.

Pleasantly steamed, my mind held down the conversation, a conversation of questions. I questioned the civilisation of a nation, a nation that had left mainland Europe centuries ago and moved to its western most island, looking for a peaceful existence, in search of a new beginning, a nation that had spent centuries fighting and driving out foes. Yes, we had won our freedom, but freedom from whom? The poor were still being evicted, small businesses still living in fear of the city sheriff, river bailiffs with jeeps and radios, catching and intimidating the unemployed young fellas as they strachauled the odd salmon from the river - people in court for robbing Christmas trees? It sounded so like the stories of the King's deer and the King's domain, it just seemed so mediaeval.

I could still hear the hum of John's conversation, he was talking about modernisation, the lunch-time trade and pub-grub. He was talking baloney, he couldn't even cope with the few auld cronies he called his regulars but, I was in so deep with my thoughts, I could only afford him the odd nod, in recognition of his efforts.

As if it were teasing out the pieces of a scrambled jig-saw, my brain threw up images of an Ireland, new and old trying to create a whole. I saw famine and food mountains, I saw Viking and tourist, I saw Meabh, Gráinne, Constance and Mary, I saw Eamon, Seán, Charles and Bert, men born to be king, men born to lead this new Ireland, men who had lost the civil war; the losers wear laurels. Here lay the problem of the solution to the Irish problem, we had losers for leaders. I saw the crosier and a people crucified. I saw abortion and freedom without choice. I saw freedom, or, was it a mere transfer of ownership? The spailpín fánach, cottier or unemployed blue-collar worker, men like me, didn't get a look-in in this new Ireland, this free Ireland. It seemed to me that our liberators, having failed to grab the bull by the horns, were now in the horns of a dilemma, and were in the process of transferring the ownership of the Irish people, land and traditions over to a greater power. My mind was in a mess.

* * * *

John's conversation came in more clearly.
"Remember dat fella, he arrived in here with you, when you came back from England that time, Mick was it?"

78

PENNY FOR YOUR THOUGHTS

On the table amongst that bunch of new small decimal coins was an old ha'penny with the Pig, still with me after all these years.

"Do ya ever see him now? John continued.
"And what's he up to at all, at all?"
"Who? Mick?" I asked, a bit dazed.
"Dat's him!" says John, "the very man!
...what's he up to?"
I stopped and gathered my thoughts.
"He's emigrated to Australia
The last I heard, he was working as a brickie.
A brickie." I repeated.
"Would ya believe that, and him a labourer.
It mus' be a great country, boi
to have a labourer workin' as a brickie...
an' over here the brickies are workin' as labourers."
I paused to take a breath.
"C'est la vie! boi," says John.
"C'est là shaggin' vie!" says I.

I looked at John, his big broad smile with not a tooth in sight, his head bent unevenly between his hunched shoulders. It seemed to me that John, too, had noticed the change in this new Ireland. We weren't exactly sure what had changed or what the consequences of such a change would be. It was a case of the less said the better. Me and John were a little long in the tooth to be getting involved in a cause. He reached deep into his pocket, pulled out a shining new £1 coin and crashed it down on top of the dirty old Pig, like a card player with a winning hand.

"Beat dat in two darts!" he shouted, and mentioned something about Lady Lavery and the vanishing paper money.

John straightened his head as best he could between his shoulders. He then lifted his shoulders uncomfortably onto his hunched back, and turned towards the bar. He muttered something about '4F' hot pub-grub snacks and the days of pig's head and crubeens being numbered.

"I suppose you'd never think of gettin' one of 'em...," I paused
"...espresso coffee makers, would ya," says I, slagging John.

PENNY FOR YOUR THOUGHTS

I picked some bacon from my teeth with the corner of my Major box
John limped back behind the bar and, as he dropped down the flip-lid
of the counter, he stopped.

"Espresso?" his voice raised in pitch and volume.

"Espresso me ass o."

John left a cackle of a laugh out of him. He threw two more
crubeens out on top of some white paper on the counter and laid off
three more pints of Murphy's. With just the top of his baldy head
showing from inside the counter, he sat down and finished reading his
paper.

The clock ticked, steam rose from the pig and the sun cut rays of
godliness through the dust and smoke. The feeling was warm and safe,
it was nice to be drinking stout, smoking Major with a bellyfull of pig. I
supped, sat back, and my mind weighed anchor, we set off through the
foam and mist, once again, on a voyage through the decades.

The Pigeon with no Hole

"You're a bar manager?"

I had visions of a future of FREE drink.

"Yep!"

He smiled smugly.

"Fully trained. How about yourself, what are you?"

His eyes pierced the bridge of my nose.

"I'm a teacher...er...fully qualified!"

I smiled.

"What do you teach?" he probed.

My smile crumbled, I explained that I was a teacher, without a class, without a school, without a job. He gave me that 'ah, shu' God love us!' look.

"Cutbacks...!"

My excuse.

My job description, well beyond its 'sell-by-date'. I was an unknown variable, no identifiable tag, an intangible asset, a pigeon without a pigeon-hole. The bar manager viewed me with suspicion. He was unsettled by my unemployment. Different things to different people, like abstract art, I was a painting without a picture. But I was me, I was free, and the drink was not.

"What bar do you manage?"

I reorganised my thoughts.

"Er...well, I'm actually between jobs at the moment. I'll probably get a few nights during the Jazz Festival."

He was humbled.

I saw him for what he was, the manager became man, we talked. Like pigeons, we spread our wings and rose into our colourful world, out of reach of the masses. We soared up there, way above their heads.

Out of Limbo

I didn't bother with a shower. You know the way that sometimes you couldn't be bothered with a shower. Well, that's how it was. I didn't have a shave either. I suppose I'd seen enough of the shower and shave routine in the old days before I found myself. Anyway, I didn't have that much time. It was now 9 o'clock and I had to get over to Crosses' Green to sign on, and then make my way back up to the North Chapel by 11 o'clock for Eddie's Confirmation.

One quick look around the bedsit - everything was off.

"I'll clean up this mess when I get back," I promised myself again, and then I stopped.

"No, the new me begins here!"

A quick run around the room, scent checking socks, underpants and armpits of garments. A black plastic rubbish bag was the fate of everything laundry bound. This way, I could kill a few birds with the one stone.

I mapped out my morning.

Drop me laundry into the launderette for around 9.30.

Cut across by the Opera House, up French Church Street, through the English Market, maybe even have a cup of coffee in Iago's.

Give myself until 10.15. Then down Tobin Street, past Triskel, over to Hanover street and sign on. I should be out by quarter to eleven. Then it would be just a simple matter of cutting across Washington Street, up the Marsh, back into the North Main street, up the North Main street, across the North Gate bridge, up Shandon street to the North Chapel, in plenty of time for the Confirmation. And, when all that fuss was over, I'd have the rest of the day to myself. Seemed like a fairly full morning for an idle man.

I threw my black plastic bag over my shoulder, took one more look around the room.

"I'll sort this place out when I get back!" I promised myself again.

Out into the fanlight lit hallway. In the darkness stood Herman, measuring tape in hand, measuring his uncut sculpture.

"Ah, Pluto! That was your daughter, yes?" As a German, he was incapable of concealing his nosiness.

"Well actually Herman, she's not really my daughter, she's me ex-girlfriend's daughter. I only fed and clothed her for a year or two."

Herman looked confused but, to be honest, I didn't have the time or energy to explain to him.

"More rubbish, Pluto?" Herman pointed at my bag of laundry.

"Laundry!" A short reply.

"You are going down town, yes?"

I explained my agenda of laundry, coffee, Dole and Confirmation.

"Wait just one moment, I go with you...I get my laundry, yes?"

Jesus! This was all I needed...I stepped out onto Waterloo Terrace, dropped my laundry bag to my ankles. I slumped there on the wall waiting for Herman, the German.

"Come on Herman boi, will ya, I'm mad late!" I left a roar out of me.

I looked down onto the geometry of Kent Station.

"Kent Station, Kent Station, Kent Station....
Kent! Kent! Kent!"

I mouthed a rhythm, always interested in sounds and rhythm. I remember once, on the Cork to Dublin train and the "clickety-clack" mixed with the ticket collector calling "Port-Laois-eh, Port-Laois-eh, Port-Laois-eh" sounded to my mind just like Pete Seeger singing "The Lion sleeps tonight." you know the part that goes, "a-wim-away, a-wim-away, a-wim-away." Well it was just like that.

Anyway, I remember at the time thinking that it must have been similar to the way Strauss composed "Tales of Vienna Woods." Seemingly it came to him as he rode through the woods on the outskirts of Vienna in an open-top, horse drawn carriage. It was like the orchestration of nature's sounds, you know what I mean, the only difference was that the song created in my head had already been composed by somebody else. Still though, interesting?

"Herman, will ya come on, I haven't all day!"

Spring had sprung and the warm life-giving sun massaged the back of my hands. My eyes drifted across the calm of the city beyond the two rivers to the silos on the quays, right over to the grassy rolling hills on the southside out beyond Togher and Ballyphehane, all the way to the Airport.

"Hermaaaannnn!" I stamped my feet.

The second floor window shot open.

"Pluto, will you ever shut fucking up! There's people round here trying to sleep!"

Brenda the brasser was obviously still awake.

"Eh, sorry Brenda, sorry, just waiting for Herman, eh, go back to sleep, eh, sorry."

Her window slammed shut. Again, I stamped my feet.

Ah yes, Kent Station down below me. The curved parallel lines of Kent Station, now that's another strange one. I always thought the principle of the railway was straight lines, you know, maximum efficiency, maximum acceleration, shortest distance between two points, that kind of stuff, it sort of makes sense. It would make ya wonder, why in the name of all that's good and holy did they build the platform at Kent Station like a banana. Must be some good reason? It must be the only mainline station in Ireland, if not the world, that's built on a bend. Interesting?

"Come on Herman!," I growled.

"I coming, I coming!" Herman thundered down the stairs.

"Keep it down, Herman boi, will ya, you'll wake Brenda."

"I sorry, I sorry!"

He stood there, two black plastic laundry bags like only a German would, one for whites, one for colours.

"Come on!" I threw my eyes towards the city and we strolled off out of Waterloo Terrace, the early morning sun throwing our long sharp shadows westward.

"Did ya ever wonder why the station was built on a bend?" I looked at Herman.

"The Travisti Brothers." He replied matter of factly.

"Travisti Brothers?", I echoed.

"Yes, the Travisti Brothers." He was indignant. "You Cork people, really! You do not know your own city! You mean to tell me you never heard of the Travisiti Brothers, yes, no?"

"Eh, I might have heard of 'em like," says I, lying through me teeth.

"The famous terraza floor layers. Travisti Brothers, Italian, yes?"

"Oh, them Travisti Brothers, yeah sure, what about 'em?"

He went on to explain how the Travisti Brothers, Gino and Mario arrived to Cork via old Papa Travisti's scrotum and learned the age-old art of terraza laying, passed down from mouth to hand over generations of Travistis. I still couldn't make the link between the Travisti Brothers' terraza laying and the bend on Kent Station platform.

"You see," Herman stopped, bringing our procession of laundry bags to a halt. He pointed down, over the wall towards the station.

"Gino, Gino Travesti ordered more terraza than the job actually required and in an effort to conceal his blatant miscalculation, he laid the floor in a semi-circle. Strange, nobody know that, yes?"

Herman was a mine of information. If I had a hat, I'd take it off to him, but naw...he'd only be getting a big head.

"And ever since that time, Gino and Mario have been laying Travisti all over Cork." Herman smiled smugly.

It's amazing what you wouldn't pick up in a day.

By the time we reached the launderette, it was about half nine. I was running a bit late and Herman, well, he was driving me around the twist. You know the way that some people are so mean?

Well, that's what Herman was like. He stood there fumbling from pocket to pocket, jacket to trousers.

"You got a rollie, Pluto?"

"No, eh, I try not to smoke 'till tea time."

"But you smoked one this morning," he wasn't going to let me off the hook.

"And why wouldn't I, I was totally stressed out. What with bells ringing, tapping on the window, banging on the ceiling and knocking on the door. What a way to face the day. Did ya ever wake up with Waterloo Sunset on yer mind."

I stretched out my right arm and strummed the fingers of my left hand across the imaginary fretboard of my imaginary sunburst red Gibson

Out of Limbo

"Dwang diddy dwang!
Diddy dwang!
Diddy dwang!
Diddy dwang!
Diddy dwang!
Bab ba ba ba ba
Ba ba ba ba ba ba
Ba ba ba ba ba
Ba ba ba ba...."

You know how it goes.
Herman dropped his laundry bags to the footpath and we stood there.

"Ba, ba, ba, ba, ba, ba,
da da da da da da, .
dada da".

Duelling banjos and imaginary guitars.
We banged out the instrumental version of Waterloo Sunset at least once...it passed the time, but I had no time to spare.
"Eh, what time does this launderette open?"
I laid down my imaginary guitar.
Herman shrugged his shoulders. It was now half nine.
"So you have no rollies Pluto?"
"I thought I told you already," I snapped.
"Is OK...is OK...I go get some. Do you want to go half on a pack?"
Herman just never gives up.
"No!" and I gave him a pound coin.
He turned and headed up the street towards the shop.
"You keep an eye on my laundry, yes?"
I just grunted and waved and sat down on my laundry bag, comfortable but stressed.
I sat there on the footpath, trying not to think of the Confirmation, trying not to think of the time, as it flew by. So I sat there thinking...

OUT OF LIMBO

"John Player Blue? Is OK, yes?" Herman was back.

He slumped down on the kerbside and drew in deep on his assembly line cigarette.

"Here, gis one o' dem!" I threw an index finger.

"But you say you don't smoke this early in the day?"

"Yeah, but I want one now, OK!"

"I never understand you Irish, full of contradictions. This will be your second cigarette that I witness...here you are."

He withdrew a cigarette from the box, "all contradictions, you Irish.

"I remember...," Herman took a drag, "when I first came to this country..."

And there the saga unfolded. It was as interesting as a dead blue bottle, all dried up in a web in the corner of an old window frame.

Seemingly, he was in Insurance or something in Dusseldorf when he heard some music. It was either the Clancys or the Dubliners or Johnny Logan or U2 or maybe the Wolfetones...anyway, it didn't matter, well, it didn't matter to me at any rate. It certainly mattered to Herman because it changed his life. He chucked the job and found his way to beautiful Bundoran in Donegal. Slowly he drifted south along the Irish coastline and found himself in Cork by the Lee, that was ten years ago.

I sat there, listening, not out of a sense of manners or interest, but because I couldn't be arsed changing the subject. All I wanted was to ditch my laundry in the launderette, if the place would ever open, get over to the Dole and back up to the North Chapel for Eddie's Confirmation. So, I sat there listening. Herman couldn't tell a story to save his life but it didn't stop him trying. He rambled on, motivating himself from near tears to loud guffaws of laughter with his own story telling.

He relished the fact that all the crucial changes in his life were brought about by pure chance. Big swinging mickey! So what? There he was, sitting on the kerb, waiting for the launderette to open. It wasn't as if he had reached the zenith of mankind with all these uncanny twists of fate. If anything, poor aul' Herman was on the scrap heap. And you know what? He didn't even know it. But then again, maybe there were things I didn't know? Maybe Herman comes from an immensely wealthy family. Maybe his family was one of those Nazi dynasties who made a fortune during the war and were able to hold onto it. Maybe this was all a bit of fun for Herman and in ten years' time he'd be sipping his brandy in a hunting lodge in Bavaria and recounting his days in Cork and how pure chance had brought him back into the family fold, back to his senses, back to his fortune. Maybe it was all a plan.

Not intending to be rude, I stood up.

"Listen Herman, I don't think this launderette's gonna open today," I reached for my black bag.

"It will open, it will open, he may be a bit late, he is often late....but it will open," Herman reassured me.

I didn't know if I was sick of waiting or worried about being late for Eddie's Confirmation, but I definitely knew I had to lose Herman. He was driving me mad.

"Listen Herman, I'm gonna head over towards the Dole, I really don't have the time to be hanging around here, well not today anyway."

"I go with you," Herman moved to get up.

"What? You're gonna come to the Dole with me? Sure, you're not signing on, you're on a Fás Scheme." I threw my eyes to Heaven.

"I have things to do in town," Herman smiled.

What could I say? So, our little parade of black plastic bags struck off, down Devonshire street, up Pine street, towards town.

By the time we reached Christy Ring Bridge, I was up to my eyeballs with Herman. A nice guy, I'm sure, but enough is enough is enough.

"Hey! Look!" Herman dropped his laundry bags.

"What?" I really wasn't interested.

"There, Herman shrieked, there!"

"Where?"

"There...there in ze river." His eyes were popping out of his head.

I dropped my bag to the pavement. It was one of the most tragic sights I had ever seen. There, in the middle of the river, was a pigeon. He was floating backwards on a turned tide, out to sea.

What was most distressing was the pigeon's apparent lack of distress. He sat there, floating backwards, looking quite content. He seemed resigned to his situation. God only knew how he got into the river, or how long his unwebbed claws battled the inevitability of the turning tide.

But there he was, floating downstream,to his almost certain doom, happy as Larry, looking around, enjoying the free ride and view.

"We must do something!" Herman was hyper stressed.

"Do something? Ya mean like jump in after him or something?"

"Nein, nein!" Herman always resorted to German when he was upset. "Vot we need is a rope or a piece of wood."

"You must be joking!" I looked at Herman.

But, before I could raise an eyebrow or lift a hand, he was gone, at a gallop, running up Lavitt's Quay to the nearest lifebuoy.

"Gone! Gone!," he ran back towards me, slapping his forehead, "ze life belt is gone..typical!"

But he didn't stop there. He kept running and running, must be contagious, 'cos I ran after him, round to the stage door of the Opera House.

Herman stood there flaking the door.

"What?" The door shot open.

"A bird! In ze river!"

Herman explained the plight of the pigeon in the best pidgin English he had. I can only guess that the guy in the Opera House understood him perfectly because, before I knew it Herman was off again, running up Lavitt's Quay, but this time he had a 12 foot, 3 x 2 under his arm and, like a knight in shining armour he charged. I followed on, carrying the bags of laundry, Sancho Panza-ish.

* * * *

"Ah no! You must be joking, Herman!"

"No joke, Pluto, now, hold onto my jacket." And he climbed over the railings of Patrick's Bridge.

"Now," he grunted, "I will guide zat poor pigeon over to ze quayside with this stick and we can save him at ze steps, yes?"

"Eh, I dunno Herman, I dunno".

"Alright...alright...here he comes." Herman stretched as I held on, knuckles whitened.

"Now! Now!" he lunged forward. "Now!"

A valiant effort, but he missed by a mile. I grappled with Herman. He rotated the full 360, dropped his 3 x 2 to the footpath and climbed back over the railings of the bridge to safety. He took off, running to the far side, dodging traffic, like someone possessed. By the time Herman took up his position inside the railings, the pigeon had floated out of reach. We stood there, watching as the pigeon bobbed up and down, not a care in the world. I couldn't help feeling an empathy with that pigeon. I understood the freedom experienced when one accepts the inevitability of destiny but Herman was not so philosophical.

"The Animals' Home," he pointed in the direction of the Bus Office.

"Zey may have a net or something, yes?" and once again he ran. At this stage, I was wrecked from all the running, and anyway, it was getting late.

By the time I caught up with Herman, he was beating down the door of the Dogs' Home.

"Tis useless, Herman. This place don't open for another 10 minutes. By then the pigeon will be halfways to Cobh."

"Quick! To the docks! We will get something there for sure. Come on, quick. We will catch that pigeon at ze next bridge."

And once again, he was off, running like a lunatic down past Carey's Tool Hire, down beyond the Idle Hour, down among the hoppers and silos, and I, like a bigger lunatic, following him.

* * * *

He wasn't very tall, but he was built like a brick. I'd guess he had just fallen out of one of the early morning houses. He stood there in his donkey jacket and hobnail boots.

Herman made a beeline for him.

"Wha'? A pigeon?" The docker scratched his head.

"Yes, yes...he is drowning!" Herman was relieved at last to be understood.

"Drowning?" the docker swayed.

"Yes" Herman gasped, "there in ze river" he pointed manically.

Gasping for breath, holes burnt in my lungs from the fags, I stood there awe-filled as Herman the artist explained the plight of the pigeon to this legless docker. It was the United Nations at its best. The docker swayed and nodded and shook hands with Herman.

"So, we get some rope, yes?" Herman waved his hands in the air.

"Why?" enquired the docker.

"For ze pigeon." Herman was indignant.

"Sure, what's another pigeon?" The docker threw his arms in the air and staggered off in the direction of the Marina bar.

I was inclined to agree with the docker. What is another pigeon? And that's where I left Herman and his two bags of laundry, pleading with the drunken docker.

Anyway, today was a big day for me, it was Eddie's Confirmation and I was running a bit late.

Come Out Now!
Hacker Hanley

"**S**ín amach do Lámh!"

Brother Murray roared, blood pressured eyes bulging. My right hand shot out for three strokes of martyrdom. Brother Murray, had taught me all I knew about martyrs, and here he was persecuting me.

You see, Hacker Hanley was spreading it around the school yard that there was no Santy Claus. I knew he was wrong, so, with the strength of faith instilled in me by the Christian Brothers, I answered the call. Emotionally I jumped, faith inspired, to defend Santy's honour. I didn't do a good job of defending him. Within fifteen seconds, I had a bloody nose, split lip, black eye, and Brother Murray was frog marching myself and Hacker, by the scruff of the neck to the office. I protested my innocence, proclaiming defence of the faith ...

"Sín amach do lámh eile!"

Three more lashes on my left hand, martyrdom came quickly and easily to the faithful.

That first autumn in the big school dragged. A place where justice was dispensed painfully and systematically, with no course of appeal. But Christmas drew close, spirits lifted, and time flew. Hacker had planted the seeds of doubt about Santy. I had heard the rumours, and noticed the tell-tale discrepancies. But, all in all, my faith in Santy was strong, strong but questionable.

* * * *

Christmas arrived and the house was mad. Tucked up in bed, squealing with excitement, we listened to the radio. Santy had just signed off from the North Pole, he was on his way.

"Shut up! or he won't come at all. An' if he does, he'll only bring ye lumps a' coal!" my big sister calmed us, issuing seasonal threats.

Threats or no threats, there was no controlling us, final warnings were roared from the kitchen downstairs, and then the final solution. It was the oldest trick in the book, 'divide and conquer', oppressors of the world unite. I was put out to the guest bedroom, out in the extension, miles away from my brothers and sisters. I lay there in that strange bed, with its shampoo-smelling, hard sheets for what seemed like an eternity listening, thinking ....

It never snowed down Coburg Street, but Christmas spirit was thick on the ground. Outside, a lone drunk was murdering 'White Christmas' and gangs of fours and fives hammered out a rhythm on quarter irons to the tune of jingle bells, backed by a devilish chorus of howling and roaring. In the distance, my brothers settled, I listened. My strange bed warmed. In a semi-dream world, my head filled with meandering thoughts and sounds ... and I drifted ... to timelessness.

* * * *

I was snapped back to reality by the sound of somebody moving about at the top of the stairs. Terror ran through my veins. If it was my mother and she found me awake, I was in trouble, but if it was Santy Claus, I was in big trouble. Pretending to be asleep, I turned to the wall, eyes clenched tightly shut. Footsteps shuffled along the hall and stopped outside my door. The handle turned, the door eased open. I was petrified, eyes clenched and hyperventilating. Whoever it was crept around the room behind me. I sensed somebody towering over me, breathing down on top of me. My heart was pumping, chest, toes and ears pulsating. A firm hand came heavily down on my shoulder, gasping for breath, I turned, and there he was, ...
"Fa, Fa, Fa....Father
Ch..., Ch..., Ch....Christmas
'S dat you Father Christmas?"
I stumbled over the words.
"Fadder Cristmus?" his voice rose in pitch.
"Don't mind your Fadder Cristmus, my name is Santy, boi!" he introduced himself indignantly, in the flattest Cork accent you ever heard.

"Santy boi?" I echoed.

"No, no, not Santy boi! Santy Claus, boi!"

"Oh, Santy Claus boi!" I corrected myself.

"Das right! Santy Claus boi!"

And sure enough, there he was in the flesh, Santy Claus boi.

I must admit, he didn't fulfil my expectations. Well, he was only slightly overweight, no flowing white beard, only the grey stubble of two days' growth. Not a particularly jolly character, he wore a brownish/red duffel coat and a well worn pair of black, steel toe-capped, work boots.

"Wha' are you gawkin' at, I haven't got all night boi. I'm having fierce trouble with me goory, 'tis up on de flat roof!" he pointed to the ceiling.

"Me back axle is seized, one of me bridles is banjaxed, an' you're de only man I could turn to."

"Me?" I shook with disbelief.

"Das Right!" he reassured "You! I saw how you handled Hacker Hanley!"

Handled Hacker? I thought to myself. My memory of the incident had Hacker handling me, and not with kid gloves either, but who was I to argue with Santy.

"An' I saw how you stood up to Brother Murray. You're de man I want in my corner."

Well I was out of my bed, into my dressing gown and up them stairs in two shakes of a reindeer's tail.

The roof glistened with a dusting of soft, white snow, and there, lined up in pairs were the reindeer, harnessed to a sleigh carrying more toys than Kilgrews window. It was majestic.

"Rudolph, Prancer, Dancer, Dorner, Blitzen ..." I mouthed the reindeer names.

"What are you on about, boi?" Santy stopped me mid-sentence.

"The Reindeer!" I replied.

"De Reindeer? Do dey look like Reindeer to you?" he was not amused.

And sure enough, there in front of me was the strangest array of beasts I had ever seen.

"Rudolph's for real." Santy continued, "de only reindeer of the pack. Dis is de great, great, great, great Granddaughter of the first Rudolph, give or take a few greats!"

They smelt strong, with muck and snow caked into their fur. Santy went on to explain that the beasts were from the eight corners of the earth, hand picked for their fitness, intelligence and skill in traversing their own particular terrain. He had a moose from Canada, called Chuck, a Sika deer from Japan by the name of Kin Chung, from Africa, a Gazelle named Naboa, a camel from the Sudan called Midhad, Rodriguez, a llama from South America, from the Italian alps, Salvatore, a mountain goat and finally, leading the pack, Finbarr, an Irish red deer.

"Hand picked ...All hand picked!" Santy repeated.

"Finbarr? ... from Ireland!" I thought to myself as I rubbed Finbarr's nose.

"Hoi! ...What about me bridle!" Santy interrupted my gloating.

"Well I can't fix it," I said, examining the worn leather, sure I know nothing about bridles!"

"Useless!" Santy threw his eyes to heaven. "A waste of time!"

"But you know what Santy?" I said, thinking aloud, "O'Connors funeral home, next door had horses years ago! Maybe they have some old bridles hanging up somewhere? And actually, now that I think of it, Daly's Garage...."

"Daly's Garage?" he questioned.

"Yeah, Daly's, down Pine Street, they'll probably have a jar of grease for your back axle."

"Me Dazza!" he smiled and clicked his fingers.

"Your head wasn't made for a hat!" and, with a hop and a skip he launched himself into the air, with the agility of a ballerina, and glided across the lane that separated our house from O'Connors, snow falling from his boots, like star dust.

"You organise de presents for de boys an' girls," he instructed, and then vanished down O'Connor's sky light.

I busied myself preparing little bundles of toys and lined them up along the roof, street by street.

"Fair dues to ya boi!" Santy was back.

"I got me bit of a bridle wrong colour though. But, what Finbarr don't

know won't bother him."
I volunteered to fix the bridle, Santy was off over the roofs, delivering, returning regularly to refill his sack.

* * * *

The bridle repaired, Santy was back from his final delivery. By the look on his face, I knew there was something wrong.
"Come here to me?" he growled
"Wha' about Hacker's presents?"
"Hacker? Hacker Hanley?" I questioned,
"Sure he's a bad boy! Surely he's on the black list!"
"Black list!" Steam thundered from Santy's nose.
"Yeah! de bad boys black list!" I repeated,
"Lump a' coal brigade!"
"Dere's no bad boys' black list!
Dere's no lump a' coal brigade," he looked disillusioned.
"Sit down dere!" he said quietly, pointing to the roof.
He sat next to me, and, there in one sentence he explained the essence of Christmas.
"Dere are two types of people in dis world.
Dose dat believe and' dose dat don't believe." he paused.
"Now! ...
I have enough on me hands trying to please the
believers than to be bothered bringin' lumps a' coal
to the unbelievers!
Now, get up dere and get Hacker's bundle together."
Between us we made up a special bundle of toys for Hacker, and Santy was off on his final round.

* * * *

His work in Cork completed, Santy gave a final check to his bridle, harness and back axle.
"Before ya go Santy!" I interrupted,

"Meself and me brothers have laid out a bottle a' Murphys and a slice of cake for ya."

"A bottle a' stout!" He looked at me as if I had two heads.

"I only work one day a year and it's the one day I get a rake of free drink. Sure, I can't drink on Christmas Eve. I couldn't be locked out a' me skull and flying around de sky? I'd be a danger to myself not to mind anybody else!"

"But ya must get hungry?" I butted in.

"Hungry?..." A glint came to his eye. "Sure I'd often take a slug of a bottle of milk or tear a leg off a freshly cooked turkey. Dere's many a cat, got no Christmas dinner because of a turkey leg I had eaten. But, speaking of food, I must call over to Noreen Griffin's."

"Noreen Griffin?" I thought to myself.

Noreen Griffin and her brother Denis ran a café and cake shop across the road.

"Noreen's too big for Santy!" I protested.

"Noreen's a believer!" Santy whispered "And what's more, she makes de best apple tarts in Cork. In Cork?" his lips broadened "In de world! I'll be back in a minute."

* * * *

On his return from Noreen's, we made ready for the next leg of the journey. He was heading west to Allihies, where Finbarr the Irish red would switch places with Chuck the moose and then, on to Newfoundland.

"Keep de setting sun in sight an' the morning won't creep up behind ya! Das how it's done, boi."

He revealed the secret of global travel in one night.

We pushed the sleigh so that it stretched diagonally across the roof, giving it room for take off. Santy climbed aboard. I settled Finbarr, rubbing between his antlers. I didn't want him to go, but there was a job to be done.

"Will ya call again?"

I sniffled, trying to hold back the tears. He called me to his side.

"De day you stop believing in me is de day I'll stop callin' to you. Are ya right dere Finbarr!" he tugged the bridle.

* * * *

They had lightening in their eyes, and fire in their breath, as their hooves thundered off across the roof, and up and away the sleigh lifted to the stars, knocking sparks off MacKenzie's gutter as it rose. They circled overhead.

"Give something nice to me Aunty Kit and Jack in Adrigole." I shrieked.

"You're a sound man!" he roared from the circling sleigh. "One of our own!"

It was at that moment, as the moon lit up his hood-darkened features, it struck me that Santy was the head off Brother Murray. And like Brother Murray, there was a tough job to be done, and he was the man to do it. Santy circled the sleigh one more time, he rose the whip up above his head and laughed as it cracked over Finbarr's antlers. And with a roar of, "Come out now! Hacker Hanley!" he was gone, shooting across the southern sky, westward.